Then My Eyes Were Opened

For Edna — I appreciate your friendship, your empathy and your clear memory of "how it used to be". So much ♥ thank you for the story about my beloved Aunt Birla, and that you are a part of my book. (page 107)

2007

Clara Wallace Nail

Clara Wallace Nail

PublishAmerica
Baltimore

First printing

At the specific preference of the author, PublishAmerica allowed this work to remain exactly as the author intended, verbatim, without editorial input.

ISBN: 1-4241-9115-7
PUBLISHED BY PUBLISHAMERICA, LLLP
www.publishamerica.com
Baltimore

Printed in the United States of America

Dedicated to the
Emmanuel Sunday School Class
of Locust Grove First Baptist Church
for their love and support
as we serve our Lord Jesus together,
and especially to
Alice Fendley Martin,
special reader and encourager.

Acknowledgments

To Dr. James N. Griffith I give special thanks for his immeasurable help and encouragement in the early preparation of this manuscript.

To Ramona Beshear for great proofreading and helpful suggestions.

To my brother-in-law, Robert Nail, for refreshing my memory of farm related measures, and for much assistance with plows and sweeps.

To JT and Phyllis Gilbert and family for their friendship to my husband, and all the help given me after he was gone.

To the Reverend James H. Miller, spiritual advisor and friend to my husband and me.

In memory of Helen Minter, a wonderful mentor.

To Orion Jenkins Holder and the late Gene Holder, who recommended Publish America, and for those writer conferences we attended together.

To each of the following pastors and their wives, who through the years have been my spiritual leaders:

The Reverend Merrill Meadows
The Reverend Bill Allison
The Reverend John Yarbrough
Dr. and Mrs. Howell Upchurch

The Reverend and Mrs. Byron Gibson
The Reverends Harold and Dorothy Bell
The Reverend and Mrs. Bill Mendum
Ret. Navy Chaplain and Mrs. Dudley Prickett
Dr. and Mrs. Guy Sayles, Jr.
The Reverend and Mrs. Kenneth Haag
The Reverend and Mrs. John Jenkins
Ch. (Col.) A.M. Moore III and the late Mrs. Moore
Dr. and Mrs. Craig Bowers

My appreciation to my children: Wayne E. Nail for his gift of editing, and Brenda Nail DeLauder for casting light where I most needed it. My blessings to both of them for aiding me in presenting this work.

Contents

*Then My Eyes
Were Opened*

Chapter 1
The Road to Emmaus

"As they talked and discussed things with each other, Jesus himself came and walked along with them; but they were kept from recognizing him" Luke 24:15-16 (NIV).

"And beginning with Moses and all the Prophets, he explained to them what was said in all the Scriptures concerning himself" Luke 24:27 (NIV).

"When he was at the table with them, he took bread, gave thanks, broke it and began to give it to them. Then their eyes were opened and they recognized him, and he disappeared from their sight" Luke 24:30-31 (NIV).

I have long been intrigued with this story about the two men walking along on their way to the village of Emmaus. A peaceful, ordinary scene with them discussing the current news that had just exploded over Jerusalem. I think the story has perhaps the greatest impact of any of those following the resurrection of Christ.

Every one of us is on that road. We may not be going to Emmaus, but the name is as good as any so let's call it that. Life is an Emmaus Road. We are all going somewhere, we have been going somewhere all our lives just because we were born and inhabit this planet.

I see three great truths depicted here which embrace each of our lives. The first one: Whether we personally "know" Him or not, Jesus is with us in this life. We may never see Him, we may never feel His presence, we may not even later when we look back, realize that it is so. But He is there.

The second truth: Not until we are ready will our eyes be opened to enable us to recognize Him.

The third truth: Through the happenings along the way we can be opened to greater understanding of who and why we are. He will teach us many things through those who travel with us.

Younger, I had no inkling of the power, the protection, the peace and security that walked daily with me. My heart may have burned within me and I thought it was indigestion.

I only know one day the dazzling realization flooded over me that as I stood there looking down the years, I saw Him clearly. In the lives of those who walked certain distances with me, I could at last see some of those things He taught me through them. It was not always people who walked with me. Sometimes when I was absolutely alone He drew lessons for me through beloved animal friends or from His creations in nature.

My road has been crowded with many familiar faces, who gave support and love and hold a special place in my heart. But herein I use encounters in which I was granted some particular insight. For the most part only first names are given because it is Jesus who is the central figure, whose teaching is the focal point in each story. While much of my very ordinary life is behind me, I look forward with anticipation and joy to the divine appointments He has yet prepared for me.

Now it is your turn to look down your own Road to Emmaus. In order to see Him more clearly, if you have not already done so, there is yet time for you to embrace Him. Welcome the Lord Jesus into your heart. When He "breaks the bread" of truth before you, your eyes will be opened.

Chapter 2
The Storm

On a strangely warm day in November when our children were small I came around a great bend on the road to Emmaus. The morning began like many others. My husband had gone to work, and our youngest was asleep in her room. Her brother, a first-grader, was getting ready for school.

Dark clouds were gathering as a foreboding stillness hovered over us. My attention was drawn to a different sound, a peculiar roar bellowing down a long tunnel. Suddenly, frenzied activity burst forth outside with powerful gusts of wind.

I hurried to our daughter's room. Just as I stepped inside, one of the windows crashed to the floor. Torrential rain swept around us as I gathered my little girl into my arms. My son followed close behind me but neither child so much as whimpered. I led us to the center of the house, terrified as what to do. At that precise moment a Presence filled the room, a powerful sensation of safety and serenity. A strong impression to sit beside the inner wall flooded my mind.

Without question I placed Brenda in the little hall and Wayne and I knelt beside her. From the sound outside, I knew many things were affected, but I felt protected. Then as quickly as it had come it was over—calm and still.

Our barns formed a semi-circle around the yard and house on the east and south sides. Outside debris was everywhere. One barn was completely demolished, from the two others heavy tin roofing curled like massive wood shavings was spread across the yard and field. The shingles on the south side of the house were laid back like a giant coverlet. Beyond the barns to the east, eleven trees of our small apple orchard were wrenched completely out of the earth.

My husband came home to make repairs requiring immediate attention. We were unharmed, the children more surprised than frightened. Wayne went on to school; I prepared my preschoolers breakfast. The day's routine was once again set in motion. Later I would re-examine the experience of that morning and the Presence who came as suddenly as the violence.

Even before I became active in church and before I found Jesus as my Savior, I believed there was God. I said the child's prayer Mama taught me; I memorized the Lord's prayer because Nannie said I should.

When I was taught that Jesus is God's Son and He gave His life for me, I believed it. At thirteen I joined the church on that premise and was baptized. Something I couldn't explain happened to me then; I knew I was different inside. I felt I was filled with light, that any darkness within was penetrated by this light.

But I had not experienced such an awareness of a Personal Presence as I did on the day of the storm. Was it just a feeling? Imagination can do powerful things to you, especially when you're scared half to death.

I knew, however, down at the core of my very being it was not imagination. No doubt about it, we were protected. It was a sobering experience to view the devastation left behind, and to realize we had been completely shielded. I recalled how quickly the Presence had come with comfort and calmness during the most terrifying moments, not after the wind's onslaught had ended.

I thanked God for sparing us from injury, but I also questioned, "Is there more? What am I to understand?" I was familiar with answered prayer. When we were still childless I had received a specific promise. This was different. It was almost like I received a summons.

I waited. I focused on emptying my mind, on listening. I heard no voice from heaven, but He did answer. We use words such as spoke, heard, said, when actually He impresses our minds. Over and over in my mind was the strong suggestion, "Write about the storm. Write it down."

There was no doubt I received correctly, or that it was my own idea because I was not one who shared personal and private thoughts.

I enjoyed writing picture book stories for my children. I mailed out a few of those and received some glowing letters albeit they were rejections. I didn't try again. A nicely worded rejection was still a rejection.

Nonetheless, I began to write about the storm as well as other meaningful incidents. It helped me figure things out and acted as a sounding board. Eventually I began to keep a journal. For me, only.

It would be many years before I grasped I was to share those personal encounters, let alone to actually submit any of them for publication. But the storm whipping through our farm that day was the catalyst which brought me and the written word together. I had turned a corner. And I had received a summons.

❧⧈❧

"Holy Father, I wish I had been more obedient to the summons You gave on that long ago day. The years and time seem to have run faster than me. Then, I am reminded that Your timetable is not the same as mine. Perhaps this is what You want me to share at such a time as this."

Chapter 3
Anointed

Although I wrote about the storm, I never told anybody I felt God had asked it of me. I laughed at my foolishness. Who was I, that God wanted this of me? He got my attention, but what could I write which would be of help to anybody else?

Still, I whipped out flowery phrases to paint colorful word pictures, which I was careful to tuck out of sight. At the same time there was a gnawing at me, a hunger desiring more but I didn't know how to go about it. Or even if I had anything worthy of sharing.

Then one day when I picked up the county paper the name, Dr. C. Roy Angell, caught my eye. I had read several of his books, moving collections of his sermons over a lifetime in the ministry. They were helpful accounts that motivated those who heard them, and later those who could read them.

Dr. Angell was to be the visiting speaker in the church I had attended before my marriage. Services would be held each weekday morning as well as in the evening. This was my chance to go hear him for myself. And hear was all I had in mind.

Along about then I began to receive suggestions. "This is it.

You must not only hear him but speak to him. Go. This is the opportunity you need right now."

Finally I agreed with the inner prodding, "Okay, I'll go and sit there and listen."

The voice was persistent. "That is not enough. You are to seek this man out and request his help about what you have written."

"Me? Ask a stranger for help? Never!"

"Yes. He is not a stranger to me, and you are to see him."

I decided I truly had a mental problem, but I went to the church for a morning service. I made reasonable peace with the inner voice by taking a few pages of manuscript with me.

From a pew far at the back of the sanctuary, I was impressed that Dr. Angell seemed a kindly, elderly man. I liked what he had to say. I was blessed by his books. But no, I certainly could not impose myself upon his heavy schedule.

After the service I made my way out of the church and down the street. On the inside a battle was going on. I reached the car and put forth my hand to open the door when the urge became so strong I turned around to retrace my steps. I couldn't believe I was doing this! He probably had already left the sanctuary.

At this point I seemed powerless to disobey the inner force which took me back into the church. And there stood Dr. Angell, all alone as if he were waiting just for me.

When I stammered out my interest in writing and my lack of experience, he suggested we go into the church parlor so I could tell him about it.

It is said that Dr. Angell was a man who would go the second mile to help another. He patiently listened to me. He took the time to read some of the pages I had with me. He didn't pat me on the head and say they were nice. He gave me encouragement and concrete advice, suggestions where improvement was needed, and asked if he might pray right then for me.

I had pigeon-holed him: elderly. However, hearing him talk I realized his vitality was ageless. As he took my hands in his to pray, I became aware of an electrifying charge pulsing through the parlor. I knew instinctively that the jolt of power which passed into my being didn't come from him but through him. The Presence filled me with confident hope I had never known until that moment, and which has never left me even at my lowest hour.

Dr. Angell was merely fulfilling his life long duty as God's servant. Struck too speechless to say anything more than thank you, I could understand in a new light what Isaiah might have felt when he wrote, "The Spirit of the Lord God is upon me, because the Lord has anointed me." (Isaiah 61:1 NASB)

Now I knew why God had made the appointment for me to speak to Dr. Angell. His part was to pray for me. From that brief time in his company I gained an awareness of God's power and nearness that would propel me forward to write in obedience. This was indeed some of what God wanted of me. I felt I had been anointed.

"Most Holy God, I was filled with awe at the electrifying power that came to me that day through Dr. Angell. Thank You for those times You have pushed me forward when I have been afraid and insecure. And thank You for the lasting encouragement your servant gave me on that short distance down the Emmaus Road."

Chapter 4
Beyond Myself

The pain peaked, leveled out, only to rise again and again into waves of sheer agony. Then with one final burst, icy in its intensity but swift in its relief, I heard a beautiful cry as tiny lungs gasped their first breath. Our daughter was born. The clock on the delivery room wall stood at 6:16 P.M.

How different from the arrival of our first child where every surgical preparation was made for the possibility of a difficult breech birth. With this child, also a breech delivery and only a nurse in attendance, the natural process of birth brought forth another miracle of creation.

Fully awake, alert to the power of life's beginnings, I was caught up in one of God's miracles in action. He had entrusted another precious little life into our care.

What better comparison to the human struggle with creativity! What else can touch us so deeply, take us to the highest level of travail, yet at the same time bring us to towering peaks of joy and fulfillment?

The remembrance of the physical pain has faded. But my heart and my mind still holds the magnitude of the moment when I saw this child fresh from her protective nest. In much the same way all things significant and important in our lives have a beginning point. Each purpose, each achievement had before it a time of waiting, of anticipation, of hope, of struggle before its final approach to fruition.

When I first discovered I was pregnant with thoughts and ideas that strained to be placed on paper, they too brought pain. Any birth — our dreams, our callings — does not occur without pangs of private labor, until eventually they must come to full term.

After I met Dr. Angell, the desire to write burned much like a fever. Sometimes the compulsion was so strong I wrote. But when the fever abated, I'd hide it in the freezer, under my winter socks, anywhere to get it out of sight, like a shameful malady. I knew so little how to proceed, or even to understand why what was inside me struggled to get out. I lacked comprehension about the need to place feelings and thoughts on paper.

It was beyond me. Maybe not so much that I couldn't get a handle on it, but I didn't want to. It was beyond what I could understand about myself. Even after someone else pointed out it might be a gift smoldering inside, I kept burying it under the handiest pile of laundry. At first, it was without knowledge that I was disobedient; later it became willful disobedience. I didn't have time, I didn't have learning, I certainly lacked confidence. I systematically ignored the silent urgings. It never occurred to me that God might actually want me to use words to help those who read them.

The realization came in tiny steps, but all the while I was going somewhere. I just didn't equate it to an Emmaus road, nor that the experiences I was led to record were those He wanted me to share.

To help me do this, He began to spotlight into my mind vivid scenes from the past. He opened my eyes to recognize in all those places along the way, Jesus had walked beside me. As I looked back I could see more clearly that He had been there all the time. As He is with you.

✽⟨✦⟩✽

"Forgive me, Father, that I have wasted precious hours and spent a large portion of my life trying to run from the gift You gave me. If there is yet time, I so much want to be obedient."

Chapter 5
Use What You Have

In the earlier years of my life I had only infant knowledge of Christ. I was what Paul, the apostle, called a babe in Christ. I didn't know anything about seeking His will for my life. If I had, I might not have run down strange alleys or taken paths shrouded in mystery. Perhaps it would have been a clearer, cleaner progression.

Still I am awestruck when I see how our course turns out anyway. I believe even when we've no idea where we are going, Someone does.

In my bedroom on the night before my wedding I stared at my reflection in the mirror. Aloud I said to that very young girl, "This is the last day you will be this person, the last night this will be your room, your home. When you leave here tomorrow you will be another person. You will begin a new life."

I was only eighteen. I had not known I should pray about this momentous decision. Even so, I believe with all my heart the young man soon to be my husband was in a larger plan for both our lives. An inner perception let me know it was a vast change and a course was set. The year was 1948.

Some of it was rocky and slippery. On occasion we met a mountain we struggled over; sometimes we would wonder what we were doing here. Neither of us ever seriously came to the place when we wished to travel without the other. We think it was meant to be and was for forty-seven and a half years, until "death did us part."

We started our journey in a tiny house on my husband's family farm. It didn't bother me that we had no conveniences. It was like playing house. However, I did have to adjust to working in the field. At home all I did was work in the dairy. I also had to do laundry with a washboard, use a sad iron for ironing, and cook on a wood stove. At my grandmother's someone was hired to do the laundry, iron, clean house, and do the cooking.

When Edwin left farming full time with his family and went to work for a farm machinery business, we moved to a larger house on my family's farm, closer to town and Edwin's job. I can't recall that I helped make this decision. It just seemed to happen.

Edwin began to talk to Aunt Berta about buying our house. Then suddenly all those plans were taken out of our hands. Edwin's uncle, his father's farm partner, died and it became necessary for us to move back to help with the crops already in the ground. The little house where we'd once lived was occupied so we had to move into the only other vacant house on the farm.

It didn't help that I didn't like the house at all. I agreed Edwin had to help his daddy, who I loved as well. He had welcomed me into the family from the beginning so Mr. Charlie had a special place in my heart. I knew it was a move we had to make.

Even so, this was one of our rocky places. Without a regular paycheck our finances were slimmer. As to looks and comfort the house was hopeless. With my attitude my husband was probably glad to be out all day in the field. I felt abandoned and alone.

One morning more disgruntled and unhappy than usual I

went outside to work off my frustration. At least I would be out of the house. Needing some mulch, I set off to the pine woods. Just to be there and smell the evergreens and hear the whisper of the pines in the soft breeze made me feel better. I piled the cart full of pine needles and then realized I was thirsty.

I knew where an underground spring ran into the creek so I went in that direction. Sure enough, the cold clear water was gurgling from the side of the bank. It made bubbly cheerful sounds as it rippled over the stones.

Here I knelt, leaned over, and cupped my hands to catch a cooling drink. As I watched the water fill my hands I remembered my daddy. I was four years old and Daddy and I were walking across a sunlit lawn. I recall saying, "Daddy, I'm thirsty." I saw the crinkle in the corners of his eyes when he grinned and said, "Well, we'll get you a drink."

I can see the faucet rising out of the ground where he bent down. I hear myself say, "But, Daddy, there's no cup."

Out of yesterday's memory his voice sounds strong and clear, "Then we'll have to use what we have, won't we?"

With that he cupped his hands with fingers tightly closed together. I see this kind, gentle man kneeling there with the hot sun on his back, and he is alive to me in a way death can never remove. I can feel his arms around me until they somehow merge with the arms of God.

The tears of resentment and disappointment I had bottled up ran down and mingled with the creek water as they both flowed away from me. I had not been fair. Edwin was doing the best he could. The responsibility to do the best I could with what I had was instilled within me long ago. I had just forgotten it.

I whispered a thank you to my daddy and a greater one to my Heavenly Father as I got up off my knees. Even in that ugly house I could do a lot to make things better.

And sure enough I did. Not only did I find ways to use what I had to make the place more livable, but my most earnest prayer was answered. Our son was born while we lived there, in the house where his daddy had come into this world.

My father-in-law died when his grandson was six weeks old. I am grateful we had returned to help him on the farm. The next year we made our fourth and final move into the house that was built and lived in by our children's great, great, grandparents. All along a certain plan for our lives was in progress. Although asking for guidance was foreign to me, I believe we were led to where we were meant to be.

I had long been intrigued with this house on the original family farm. While tenants lived here, occasionally Edwin would check on some of the crops. I would wait in the car and try to imagine what it felt like to be inside looking out. It was almost as if a magnetic pull was drawing me here. Farmed by his family since 1821, Edwin dreamed of calling this land his own.

We were the generation that came back to the first roots. It felt so absolutely right. It had to have been brought about by a much larger plan.

***

"Most Holy Father, I am awed by Your plans for our lives even when we are so unaware. The husband You gave me was beyond my own choosing — thank You that he was the one to journey with me toward Emmaus. This place, the promised land You led us to, wraps around me like Your arms of sanctuary. My soul bows in submission and humility for Your grace."

Chapter 6
The Hobby Show

It was time once again for the annual hobby show at our school. Some of my third grade classmates had exciting hobbies. They'd talk about their stamp collecting or their art. It seemed to me everybody had something interesting to do. Except me.

I cared for and rode my pony. My cousins and I built fabulous playhouses and even wheedled the neighbor boys into helping us. In return we aided them in exploring the gravel pit behind our house. Who had time for hobbies? We helped Granddaddy pick blackberries in the summer and hunt nuts in the woods every fall. But how could I show any of that in an exhibit?

I expect I fretted my mother a good bit trying to decide what to do. Absolutely everybody was going to enter something!

Eventually, with Mama's encouragement I decided to make candy. I'd never done it myself although I had watched Mama make fudge. After supper she added more firewood to the old cook stove, and stayed close by for support and advice. Since the exhibits were supposed to be our own, I worked hard trying to get it just right by myself, although it may have been a little rough around the edges.

Next day when our items were placed on display in the school cafeteria, I felt good about the finished product. How could I not win a prize? Maybe I was a little superior on my way back to my class room.

Afternoon classes were dismissed early to view the winners. I hurried to the lunchroom. My plate of fudge was in the same place next to a plate of beautiful cream-colored cupcakes. More precisely my plate was there but it was nearly empty. Only one or two of the cupcakes were gone but it won a big blue ribbon. My fudge had no ribbon at all!

I was crushed. At home I complained to Mama, "Why did they eat it up if it wasn't any good? It's not fair! I bet that girl's mama made the cupcakes too!"

"You don't know if that's true," Mama said. "But you are right about some things not being fair. Life is that way sometimes. Think about last night when you made the candy did you feel good about making it yourself?"

I nodded, remembering how hard I'd worked, and how happy it made me to actually make fudge by myself that was good to eat.

"I don't think," Mama said, "the judges should have eaten nearly all your candy. However, it lets you know you did a good job. Most important though is that you did the best you could by yourself, and you know what?"

I shook my head. Mama was making it better. "That's what really counts that you did the best you could."

"After Daddy was gone it seems Mama and I walked hand and hand a long way down that road alone. I am blessed and grateful, Lord, that not only did we have each other, but now I know so clearly we were never truly alone."

Chapter 7
Release the Reins

My husband always said if my worries were all laid to rest I'd turn a rock over and under it find another one. Although I would stoutly deny it, his accusation held some truth. Even after I learned the wisdom of turning things over to God, I often didn't.

Anything I could figure out for myself I didn't bother anybody else with it, not even God who surely is not interested in all our trivial problems. Or so I thought at the time. Of course, now for the big ones I sought Him in a hurry. But I'd still do a great amount of worrying and hanging on to whatever it was anyway. I could not see how to do otherwise.

Kathleen was a friend, who was far more in tune with God on a personal level than me. In our travel down a portion of the Emmaus Road she often gave me priceless insight. Once when I was struggling with a particular problem she gave me some advice. "You're trying too hard. Just let it go and the solution may come by itself." Perhaps I gave her one of my cynical looks for then she said, "The key is to let it loose."

Now how was I to do that? It implied to me lack of control. For several days the thought rolled around in my mind like a downhill runaway barrel. I even asked God what Kathleen meant without really believing He was going to tell me. But He did.

"Remember the reins" kept coming into my mind. I began to think it was fragment of a song I'd heard. Then suddenly, like I'd climbed into a time capsule headed for the past, a vivid scene unfolded from my childhood. I allowed my mind to retrace yesterday's path to a winter day in Ohio, a time when it seems the winters were more severe and lengthy.

Bright sun dazzled a brilliant landscape as my black pony, Toy, blazed a fresh trail through drifts of snow. The storm had passed and another was not expected. I was allowed to ride out alone with admonitions to return soon and not go far.

Some distance behind our house was an abandoned gravel pit, a huge canyon with high cliffs. I rode in that direction. To stand on the rim and look far below was a favorite pastime.

Forgetting everything but the excitement of the moment, I went farther than I was supposed to go. I didn't notice when the sun disappeared and the sky changed to a funny slate gray until it began to snow again. Realizing I'd been away too long, I turned to head for home.

Since I had ridden around part of the pit's rim, I couldn't just turn away from it to go home. It was necessary to ride back alongside the edge of the canyon. It was safe enough, but we were soon in a large swirling cloud of snow. It whipped and tore around us until my pony's head became only a dark blur. His earlier tracks were completely obliterated.

Children in snow country are taught early the danger of losing the way in a blizzard. Although I knew I was in deep trouble, it didn't scare me that the pit was near. What scared me was remembering tales I'd heard of people freezing to death. So I kept probing my pet along until suddenly he refused to budge. Toy had always obeyed my signals. But not this time.

He planted his stocky legs to the ground and stood firm. I dug my heels into his side urging him forward. I snatched at the leather, first in one direction then the next, not caring if I hurt his mouth. I beat at him with half frozen hands, and one of my mittens fell off. Painful truth howled at me louder than the wind. I was really scared now, and had no idea which way to go. I knew better than to get off the pony.

Instead I buried my face in his mane and began to cry. What with trying to wipe my face and push the hair from my eyes, my fingers were so numb, I dropped the reins. Almost as soon as I did Toy began to inch forward. Slowly, and with great care he picked his way. I knew one wrong move could plunge us into the canyon. I could do nothing but hang onto his mane.

He had one goal in mind — the safe, dry stable. Even though he couldn't see his way either, his innate sense of direction took us home. And that he did — when I released the reins.

"Remember the reins." The key is to let loose. Now I knew — as long as our hands, and our wills, are snatching this way and that, God does not have free rein to help us. When we loosen our willful control into His authority, He will show us what to do.

※〰(ＯＯ)〰※

"Dear Lord Jesus, even in those long ago days when I didn't personally know You, You were with me. I can see Your hands upon Toy's bridle as You led that precious animal with the burden he carried to safety."

Chapter 8
The Red Pitcher

When Daddy died, Mama and I left Georgia, returning to Ohio to live with cousins we called Nannie and Granddaddy, who were also my mother's foster parents. Perhaps it was the uprooting of my world which caused me to become fearful and blow tiny problems into much larger ones. Give me a flicker of fear and I would blow it into a roaring blaze.

Then, Nannie, who was a bulwark against any threat, would calm my fears and lessen my dread. She'd tell me, "Don't make mountains out of molehills. With God's help we can whittle this problem down to tackling size."

During those years lots of mountains needed to be reduced. The United States was in the grip of the Great Depression. While we were better off than most, there was little money for extras. Granddaddy raised what we ate and Mama helped Nannie put up jars of colorful canned goods. Nothing was thrown away. Nannie refurbished the clothes we wore, and we made our own entertainment.

Any out of the ordinary happening on our country road could turn a routine day into an occasion. One of these was the peddler we called the Dish Man.

He usually came in spring when the snows had melted into flowering shrubs and trees. From our house on the hill whomever caught the first glimpse of him would herald the news, "Here comes the Dish Man!"

I can see the soft spoken gentleman standing by his faded blue panel truck. His lanky frame leans over and opens the back doors. Nestled artfully in the straw is an assortment of colorful crockery.

If I was careful to hoard my pennies all year, I sometimes could buy a ceramic animal that held tiny plants, or maybe a mug for my milk. It made me feel important to count out the coins.

On one particular day as soon as he opened the door the red pitcher caught my eye. I knew I would never have enough money to buy it. But Nannie, who saw the longing gaze of a little girl heart, got it for me. Likely she did without something she needed. What she said was, "We'll put it on the top shelf of the cupboard to be used in your home someday."

A home someday was beyond imagination. Still, it was beautiful; bright red china, white inside, and stamped on the bottom in gold: 'Made in Czechoslovakia 1886.' I did what Nannie asked. I couldn't reach it, but occasionally I would open the door to look at it. It gave me good feelings just knowing where it was, high on the shelf. It was so big I knew it would hold a lot. It must be a foot tall!

Eventually adulthood, marriage, a home of my own were acquired, the pitcher forgotten. Hundreds of miles separated us the last year of Nannie's life, and I was unable to make my annual visit. She died that winter.

The flip-flap sound the tires made on the sections of the concrete highway as we sped over the miles chanted, "Nannie's dead, Nannie's dead." This was my first real experience with stark grief. I'd been so young when my father died, I'd only felt fear. Now that early fear was mushrooming. I was weighed down with the burden, dark and heavy. Who will comfort me now? Nannie would not be there to fix this problem.

I discovered others would fill some of the emptiness: my young husband, Mama, Aunt Berta. But the black cloud was so huge it pressed me down, crushing the breath out of me,

After the funeral I gathered together some of my belongings left at Nannies: my red wagon, little rocking chair, favorite books. Then I remembered the pitcher. I had not opened the cupboard in years so I was unprepared for the shock that met me.

The pitcher was in its place on the top shelf which I could now easily reach. It was still bright red with white inside, but it had shrunk to less than half the size I had always visualized. It was not a foot tall. I measured it, all four and five eighth inches.

No mistaking it was the same china pitcher; I was simply seeing its reality with adult eyes. When I took it down I could hear Nannie's voice in my memory quite clearly. "You see, the mountain may not be so big, after all. Even heartache can be whittled down to tackling size."

A peculiar peace began to nudge the cloud of grief slightly to one side. And somehow in the transaction I was shifting my fear, my burden, to another who could help me carry it. Jesus, the Friend she had told me about. Jesus, who could use a small red pitcher to let me know He could help me put all things in proper perspective. For all my life.

❧⟨♡⟩❧

"Lord Jesus, when I was but six or seven You knew one day You would use this small creamer to bring me the special comfort I would need. Thank You for Nannie and for the years she was granted to walk with me. Whenever I look at the pitcher it reminds me how You can help me get any difficulty down to tackling size."

Chapter 9
Granddaddy

I have an old photograph of Nannie, Granddaddy, Reba, their daughter, and my mother, who they raised. All four of them are sitting in an open topped touring car. Reba and Mama have long braids with big bows tied in back. Nannie is wearing an imposing hat with huge feathers, and Granddaddy is looking dapper in a bowler.

Often I think of Granddaddy that way, looking dapper. He was a small man with a mustache and snapping brown eyes. A bit stooped in old age, he still had those brown eyes that could look right through you.

I called him Granddaddy because that's what his grandchildren, Clarene, Helen, and Jerry called him. He was not my grandfather, but if it had not been for him I wouldn't ever have been born. When my daddy went to Ohio during the depression to take a job he saw advertised in an Atlanta newspaper, it turned out to be where Granddaddy worked.

The elder man befriended the young employee who was far from family. He took him to his house for home cooking and friendly faces. One of those faces was the young lady who lived with Granddaddy and Nannie, and who eventually became my mother. That was after she and the young fellow from Georgia became Mr. and Mrs.

My daddy lived only six years after that. I remember how sad Granddaddy looked when he would talk about his friend from Georgia. Maybe that's why I always felt completely accepted and welcome in Granddaddy's house. Maybe Mama did too; that's where she chose to go after Daddy died.

Although I don't recall Granddaddy ever hugging me or demonstrating his affection in that way, he was always there. When the snow was over my head, he would shovel a path to the end of the drive so I could catch the school bus. When I forgot to feed my pony or the rabbits, he did it.

When the Ohio River covered much of the world around it in the great flood of '37, he took me down the railroad tracks where we stood on the trestle for a sight I have never forgotten. Water covered everything except the top point of the statue in the cemetery, and the very tip top of the schoolhouse in the town nearest us. It was scary but I was safe with Granddaddy.

In the summer we would go blackberry picking. He would show me where to find the juiciest berries. In the fall we would take my pony to carry the walnut and hickory nuts we gathered in the woods.

In early spring he would show me how he started seed in the cold frames. When he planted his garden he would spade up a small one for me and help me get it started.

On hot summer nights when his grandchildren visited we would lie in the cool grass and look up at the stars. He would tell us about the big dipper and other constellations. He'd light a little smudge pot to keep the mosquitos away, and tell us funny stories that made us laugh.

One year when Clarene and I were just entering our teens

Nannie needed some apples. She decided we were old enough to go alone to the apple farm a couple of miles up Mt.Carmel Hill. Trees lined the road and every once in a while we would catch a glimpse of something in the shadows behind us. When we looked back however, nothing could be seen.

We arrived at the apple orchard safely and made our purchase. About halfway home we came across Granddaddy who "was just taking a walk" so we walked the rest of the way with him.

He had been following us all the time to make sure our journey was safely made. We never let him know that he had scared us half to death hiding every time we looked back to see what was following us. All our lives he had been our protector.

By the time all of us were gone from their house and Nannie died, he was almost completely blind. He lived with Reba then and Clarene, Helen, and Jerry became his protectors.

I think he was happy when I married a Georgia boy like Mama had. He liked my husband and I was thankful that he lived long enough to know him. Granddaddy had never been to the South, although he had always talked about it. One day Reba and Nelson loaded him, the girls, and Jerry into the car and set out for our place.

Edwin and I lived in a small house with only three rooms. But it didn't matter. I was ecstatic that family was coming to see us, especially Granddaddy. I never dreamed he would be able to come to Georgia. I borrowed beds and cots from Aunt Berta and we were all set.

My daddy's mother had been to Ohio several times to visit Mama and Daddy and of course knew Granddaddy, but they had not seen each other in many years. Aunt Berta had us all over to dinner while the Ohio relatives were visiting. My grandmother was ninety-two and in the last year of her life.

It was a moving experience to watch these two wonderful old

people together again. Each one had played such significant roles in my life. My grandmother didn't recognize the gentleman I called Granddaddy or even remember she had ever known him. He was blind and had to be led around.

He was distressed that her mind had gone. She was distressed that the poor man couldn't see. Even in their infirmities, they were the same unselfish people they had always been, thinking of others worse off than themselves.

They are just two of those that made my pathway easier. Without them I would not have existed, nor would I have been so blessed and protected.

Granddaddy went far beyond the second mile in being a friend to a young man from Georgia. He walked a long way down the road to Emmaus with the child left behind.

❧❧❧

"Heavenly Father, my heart is full of gratitude for Granddaddy who helped fill the place of my earthly father the best he could with generosity and protection. At this moment he seems so close to me I can see his sparkling brown eyes and hear his laughter. I praise You, Lord, for this memory."

Chapter 10
Brush in the Middle

We were smack dab in the middle of World War II. Every family who had a radio kept their ears tuned to the news reports. As they were all across America, many young men were gone from our area.

On the home front women joined what heretofore had been the men's workforce. Food and gasoline were rationed and the government issued little books that held rationing coupons for each individual.

Where once Uncle Bob had all the help he needed on the farm, he was forced to trade in some of his mules for a tractor. Tenant farmers had gone off to war too. Older men, plus women and children, tended the crops. In the fall students were let out of school early to help pick cotton.

My grandmother's house was a central point in the goings and comings of that busy time. Payne's Dairy, which was a family enterprise, delivered milk to a good portion of the town. Over the years, various of Uncle Bob's nieces and nephews—Tom, Manley, Mary, David, Olive, and Josephine—lived and worked at the dairy while attending school.

Starting at four o'clock in the morning, every day, seven days a week, we milked thirty to thirty-five cows by hand. There were no milking machines available. We bottled the milk and put the bottles in the icy cooler to await morning delivery. Then we rushed to the house, gobbled down breakfast, jumped into clean school clothes and caught the bus at seven thirty. In the afternoon, we had to milk all the cows again. Between milkings, we had to scrub down the milk barn and bottling room and drop cow feed down from the loft for the next cycle. On weekends we took our turns at milk delivery.

When I came to live with my grandmother, I served my time in the dairy as well, doing whatever task her daughter (my Aunt Berta) said needed to be done. Always busy, Aunt Berta drove one of the delivery vehicles, ran the household, and managed the milk house where the milk was bottled and capped.

Surely the labor shortage of that time is what began the do-it-yourself concept. Aunt Berta, who believed we could do anything we put our minds to, decided the living room needed new wallpaper. Wallpaper must not have been rationed.

In between dairy duties and milk delivery she readied the room to be transformed. Take my word for it that a narrow board placed between two ladders high up in the upper reaches of those 15 or so foot ceilings served as a very precarious scaffold indeed.

I didn't have the courage to tell her I was scared to death of heights. She cut the paper and stretched it out for the nasty paste we spread on with a big brush. The ceiling was first. Somehow we got the long strip of paper all plastered with a good portion of paste on ourselves. Next we climbed up on the board to wobble our way across the plank with arms stretched high overhead to secure the paper to the ceiling.

One look and you recognized a couple of rank amateurs at work. Consequently, between dairy and farm duties, Uncle Bob would rush in to save us from being completely glued to the wall. He let us think he knew more about it than we did and would relate what our next action should be. During one of these briefing episodes he was striving to explain the art of wielding the wide brush to smooth the paper. In frustration he admonished, "Put the brush in the middle and push!" We did and it worked. When we actually made contact with the paper and the brush in the proper way it made all the difference.

Of all that Uncle Bob meant to me, I remember this lesson best. Sometimes we have to do things we are not qualified to do. We must do them anyway, so we find the approach that works best. You can't apply the brush until you begin. But once you do, there is a way if you truly look for it.

Uncle Bob was filled with good common sense. If you were around him very long some of it was bound to rub off. After the death of his last parent, he, his brothers, and sisters were forced to sell the family farm that had been in their family since the King of England had given their ancestor a land grant. It was a sad time for them.

When I questioned him about it, he told me how he dealt with it. "When a family has finished with houses and lands, you let them go. As long as the need is there—use them to the fullest. When the time comes for them to pass from your hands it has another purpose."

The time came when I clung to that nugget of wisdom. It helped me through the trauma of selling my family homeplace. I was consumed with guilt that I couldn't hang onto it as Aunt Berta had done. However, when she was gone, not only could I not afford it, but its use for our family had ended. It had served its purpose for us ever since my great-grandfather's purchase in 1821.

That's when I remembered Uncle Bob's sensible way of

meeting a similar challenge those years earlier. In much the same way as we had applied the wall paper, I put the brush in the middle and I think he helped me push.

❧❦

"It was during my teen age years that Uncle Bob walked more closely with me down my road. I praise You, Lord, for his caring, for his kindness to me, for the everyday truths he imparted along the way."

Chapter 11
Nannie's Lamp

Nannie was not at home when I broke her little lamp. I was helping Mama clean the house. I recall how energetically I used the broom, a dangerous object in the hands of a small girl. I had not learned the knack of smoothly deploying it to the task. It seemed I had more handle than I needed. The part which stuck out from under my arm was what struck the tiny kerosene lamp. It shattered to the floor in many pieces.

Oh! How awful I felt. I knew how much the lamp meant to Nannie. It had belonged to her mother and was quite old. I could tell Mama was worried about it, too. Mama could fix most anything but she couldn't repair the lamp.

In the intervening hours until Nannie's return home, I truly suffered. I tortured myself with questions. What will she say? What will she do? Worst of all, I felt because of what I'd done it would cut off her love for me. That was the terrible part, to be cut off from Nannie's love. I didn't think I could bear it. If only I could go back before it was broken!

And then she came home. I wanted to hide, but Mama said I had to face my problem. Nannie listened when I, with Mama's support, told her what I'd done. She looked at the pieces beyond repair. She looked at my tear stained face. Miracles of miracles, she smiled and drew me close. "I'm sorry about my lamp. But I know it was an accident. Now let's not worry about it anymore."

What glorious relief! I had been forgiven. I was not cut off from her love afterall. Later I would learn what truth I had found. In a much greater way so it is with God. Nothing can cut us off from His love. Even when our lives lie broken and shattered at His feet. Even when we have committed some terrible act, that no matter how hard we try we can't change.

He sent His Son, Jesus, who will not only support us but will stand in our place. It is His blood poured out that makes our lives like they were before they were broken. That's why He came.

What glorious relief we are then enabled to feel! His love has not been cut off from us. He will hold us close and wipe our tear stained faces. If we let Him.

"Lord, I remember what an uncomfortable feeling I felt the day I broke Nannie's lamp. I wanted to change what had happened. It was my first experience with acute remorse. And my first experience with what forgiveness is all about."

Chapter 12
Moving the Stone

Although the following incident happened years ago, what we learned that fall morning became the means for us as a family to move many obstacles in our path.

At the kitchen sink, up to my elbows in sudsy water, I was mentally "up to my elbows" in a current problem. Mulling over a possible solution I was disturbed by sounds coming from outside where my two preschoolers were playing. I hurried to the door. What I'd heard was a truck from the County Work Camp. The prisoners were loading rocks from the recently scraped dirt road onto a flatbed truck.

The children stood under the big white oak whose already changing late summer leaves rustled in a puff of wind. The sun filtering through the foliage made kaleidoscope patterns on their backs. I smiled at their statue-like silence. Their attention was completely riveted on the activity before them.

It was a wonder Wayne, our vocal five year old, was not plying the men with half a million questions. He came equipped with an insatiable desire to learn all the whys as fast as possible. Perhaps the prison uniforms had struck him speechless. His sister, Brenda, at three seldom got the opportunity to say much. However, you could see her little mind fairly soaking up knowledge. When she made a move, you knew she'd given her best thought to figuring it out. Silently.

It didn't occur to me to hustle them inside for fear of the prisoners. Back in that more tranquil time even the men at the prison farm didn't pose any particular threat. They would not be doing road work if they weren't trusties.

Suddenly my attention was drawn to four of the men who were struggling to lift a large boulder onto the truck. I counted them, there were definitely four. They tried and tried. Unsuccessful, they left that rock in the red dust by the side of the road.

The truck moved slowly on. Wayne and Brenda stood at their post until it was out of sight. Satisfied that they were all right, I returned to my sink full of dishes and my problem solving.

A little later when I checked to see where they had gotten to, I could not immediately take in what I was seeing coming up the driveway. For trundling along on their red wagon was a huge rock! Wayne was in front, both hands manfully grasping the wagon's tongue. Brenda, bent over, was pushing it from behind. Their treasure, much too large to fit into the wagon, balanced rather precariously on top.

It couldn't, of course, be the same boulder. It wasn't possible. Four men had not been able to lift it. I hurried down the steps. My glance toward the road told me it was indeed the same rock. "How on earth…?" I began.

"We got it, Mama. In the wagon." Wayne proudly announced. True, he was a sturdy fellow with a healthy dose of confidence. That would be in his favor. Still….

"I see you did, but how on earth?!" I began again.

Brenda, always the practical one, explained, "We put the wagon under."

"Under?" I faltered.

Wayne continued, "We put the wagon in the ditch and rocked it in with a stick. It just went over."

Of course! With no knowledge of the procedure, they had let leverage do the work for them! By some miracle they had achieved the proper balance. I did not see them do it, but I knew my children. If there was any way to accomplish what they wanted done they would figure a way to do it. (To this day when the two of them join forces, it boggles the mind at what they can do together.)

I realized their success in this endeavor had something to do with motivation, as well. Obviously rock moving held little interest for the prisoners, whereas it became a challenge to the small onlookers.

Later when I returned to the house I looked up the word "leverage" to ascertain if I had correctly identified its usage. Indeed I had. One definition of leverage is: 'an increased power of action.'

Now, these many years later every time I step upon that stone to enter a room in our barn I am reminded how on that special day the children walked with me down the Emmaus Road. On many such occasions we all traveled together.

Although I was not aware of it then, Jesus was there with my young ones when they loaded their wagon. He was there with me when much later I wrote it down.

For I believe God gave this special event in our family for a reason. It has given us solutions to eradicating many problems that are workable for anyone. To remove whatever it is, be it mountains, or rocks, or even unnecessary gravel, we remember we must first be motivated. Next we study every angle. There is always a way. Then together we apply whatever leverage is necessary.

And beyond that, and while I don't imagine my little ones prayed over the rock, I have learned that prayer is the essential ingredient in getting any task done.

In fact, I firmly believe that particular leverage is what gives us the "increased power of action."

❧

"When I look down the road, Lord, at where I have already been I am filled with awe at the reality of Your Presence. Thank You for these wonderful children who walked along with me, and for that special lesson with the stone."

Chapter 13
A Little Ceramic Hand

Brenda was only ten when she first took part in the annual youth program at our church. She was much younger than the other speakers, all teenagers.

It was the year she chose to follow Jesus. I was proud that she wanted to participate, although I worried about her fitting in with the others. But our daughter was serious about being a Christian, and chose "Faith" as her subject.

Privately, I questioned her ability to write an effective speech on such a deep subject. When I suggested how she might go about it she said, "I know what I'm going to say."

I soon realized Brenda wasn't the least worried about her speech. She had no intention of writing it. Far more interesting things claimed her mind, such as riding her bicycle or catching polliwogs down at the beaver pond. Paperwork was something to avoid. In the meantime her big brother was studiously working on his theme.

The big day arrived with our youngest still minus the first written thought. I urged her, "I think you should make a few notes." Trying not to alarm or undermine her confidence, I

THEN MY EYES WERE OPENED

explained, "Sometimes when we stand before a group of people and they look back, it scares us. We may forget what we meant to say. A word or two on a card helps us remember."

As if I had not heard before, she stated more emphatically, "But, Mama, I know what I'm going to say."

When time came to go to church, I was filled with apprehension. I fully knew an embarrassing experience in one so young could be devastating. I also knew I would be scared to death without the support of something on a piece of paper to jog my memory.

Brenda didn't seem nervous at all. She carefully chose the blue dress I had made her for Easter, and took extra time brushing her hair. By now panic would have set in with me. However, she beamed with cheerful confidence as she climbed into the car with her new red Bible tucked under her arm. I noticed she also carried another small object. It was the ceramic imprint of her hand we had made together when she was four. But I didn't ask any questions. At this point I decided she was on her own.

All the speakers were good including her brother, who had used an outline for his talk.

Brenda's name was next on the printed bulletin. My heart gave a fearful mother-hen thump. I wanted to hide for her and for myself as well. Instead, I tried to concentrate on how blue her eyes were when she had that determined look.

Marching to the front as if it were something she did every day, she took her place before the congregation and began, "Sometimes I'm scared. One day I was lying on my bed thinking about being scared, and I got my Bible and read something."

She paused to open her Bible and read, "In the beginning was the Word, and the Word was with God, and the Word was God."

I let out a little breath. So far, so good, but what could she say about Scripture I didn't fully understand myself?

Pushing unruly bangs from her eyes, she looked at the audience quietly for a moment, aware she had their attention. "Since I came to know Jesus, I've learned a lot of things. This time it seemed like He was telling me if I can get what He says down in my heart, it's the same as God being there. So I don't need to be afraid anymore. None of us do, 'cause He'll help us with most anything. But we got to believe it first."

By now you could have heard the tiniest pin drop. Throughout the congregation there was complete silence, listening silence. She picked up the ceramic hand. Holding it high, she placed her ten-year-old hand over the smaller replica. "This is a print of my hand when I was four years old. That's when I didn't know much about it, and I had only a little bit of faith. Now my hand is this much bigger, and my faith is this much bigger too. What about yours?"

I huddled down in the pew wondering if anybody needed that miniature message as much as I did. I had completely forgotten the most important thing of all! I had not only doubted my child's ability, but I had doubted God in her. Her life was not yet cluttered with doubt and self- consciousness. Therefore, God's Holy Spirit was more free to help her with "most anything." She counted on that. No notes required.

And I…I had discovered how faith can beat fear any old day.

※≫(✠)≪※

"You have always been with the children and me on our road, Lord. Thank You for this child and her close walk with You, and what she has taught me. Has not Your very Word said, "a little child shall lead them."

The above chapter on faith minus the prayer was first published in *Home Life* magazine November 1982, under the title "The Day Faith Beat Fear".

Chapter 14
An Old, Faded Ribbon

Shortly before Christmas each year Edwin would herd his family into the car and we'd head for the Farmer's Market. Here he would buy cases of apples, oranges, grapes, and all the goodies people associate with Christmas feasting.

At first I could not understand why we needed cases of anything, but my husband wanted to be sure we had plenty of everything. Maybe it went back to a time when you were lucky to get an orange or an apple in the toe of your Christmas stocking. It was just the thing you did, and of course, you shared.

It had become our family custom on Christmas Eve to deliver to our less fortunate neighbors boxes of fruit, candy, cake, and a personal gift for each one. That's what Christmas is all about isn't it...giving? We gave, but we didn't receive. We didn't expect to.

That evening we drove into the last yard. While my family waited in the car, I approached Lena's house. Lena was very old, although I didn't know how old. Her mind was still clear as a bell, her will still strong. She had meant a lot to the Nail great-uncles before us. She expected us to come on Christmas eve. As she held the door open for me, I thought she looked more frail than usual.

After I listened to what she told me she had done in preparation for the holidays, I decided she was only tired. She pointed to the concrete block wall she had cleaned, careful not to disturb her treasure, the collage Wayne had made for her from bits of cloth and paper. Our son and Lena enjoyed a special rapport ever since he was a year old.

She had scrubbed her plank floor. She had cleaned off her cluttered table. All these things I duly noted, but I could tell she expected me to notice something else. I looked around the shabby room, dimly lit by an overhead light bulb. Then, on a table in the corner I spotted the only bright spot in the bleak surroundings.

It was a bright bunch of pyracantha branches with colorful berries, tied with a faded red ribbon, and artfully arranged in a fruit jar. I began to tell her how nice it looked, how it brightened up her room.

That was what she wanted me to notice. She seemed to beam when I began to praise its beauty. I was dismayed when she picked it up, thrust it into my arms and said, "This is my gift for you."

I almost blew it; I almost opened my mouth to say, "Oh no, you must keep it yourself." But the Holy Spirit gave me a good nudge and I found myself saying with more grace than I could ever muster on my own, "Why, thank you Lena, I shall enjoy and cherish your lovely gift."

On the way home I held it in my lap and carried a warm glow inside that arises from special experiences like this one. We had been given the widow's mite. She had shared all she had.

This is what Christmas is all about. It is a time of giving, but it also is a time of receiving. There is so much pleasure in giving we should never take away the joy from the giver. This was the joy Edwin received when he went to the Farmer's Market. This was the joy Lena received when she lay her gift into my arms.

This was the gift God gave on that night in a lowly stable...the greatest gift to mankind, His Son. It is this gift that cause the angels in heaven to rejoice when we receive Him.

⁂

"Holy and Wonderful Father, thank You for the experience of cherished moments like this one. From the time of Your greatest Gift to mankind, each year we honor that special night with our gifts of love to each other. I praise You for showing me first of all how to receive Your gift, the Lord Jesus, and for His teaching me the gift of receiving."

Chapter 15
Munnie

I had been married about a year when my grandmother at ninety-one fell and broke her hip. Aunt Berta and I rushed to the hospital in Atlanta to be with her, not realizing one of us needed to stay the night. We soon were aware that the medication they had given, instead of sedating her, had reacted in the opposite way. She kept trying to get out of bed so I volunteered to stay.

I had not gone prepared. Of course, we are never prepared for emergencies which wind their unwelcome ways into our lives. It would have been helpful at least to have had something to read. While the doctor had given permission for me to spend the night, it was apparent the nursing staff wasn't overjoyed at my being present.

I was young, inexperienced, and easily intimidated. I remember it as the longest, darkest, most uncomfortable night I ever spent. It was a far cry from the reclining chairs most hospital's provide for families today. There was only one hard, straight back chair in the room. Not that I got to sit much; mostly I stood at my grandmother's bedside trying to dissuade her frantic attempts to get out of bed.

I still remember it as a long, dark night, and over the years have referred to it as the dark night of my soul. For at one point I felt pretty much abandoned by God. I'd pray and then I'd watch the window, longing for the first light. I recall thinking, "Morning light will never come. This is forever. I'll just sit here on this hard chair, and that window will be dark, and nothing will ever change."

Of course, it did change. After a thousand years or more the very faintest glow began to appear. It grew and grew and finally the sun just seemed to explode into the room with its glory! Day did arrive. God had not left me in the dark forever. The night had ended. On that day they put a pin in Munnie's hip and she lived for another year.

The only grandparent I ever knew, Abi Crabbe Wallace, came by the peculiar name Munnie when I first began to identify family members with words. She was already in her seventies when I, her only grandchild, was born. My daddy and Aunt Berta had called their grandmother Muttie. Their attempt to teach me to use the same term failed miserably. Apparently, my determined personality was already taking form. The title I gave her was Munnie, and it stuck.

When the Union Army raided McDonough during the Civil War, little Abi Crabbe was four years old. Her mother watched in horror as one of the invaders lifted her child from the bed to see if money or other valuables might be hidden underneath the mattress.

Her growing years fell into the time slot when the South was rising from the ashes of defeat. But arise they did. Her people brushed off destruction and began anew. It may have played a major role in welding steel backbones to the ladies of that era. Munnie was an example of the most genteel of women, yet with an iron strength that kept her going on in the face of whatever obstacles life presented.

When her husband died in the influenza epidemic of 1918, she took over his job as Tax Receiver of the County. Her son was given the title but she was the one who did the work and held it together at the same time she was equally yoked with her sons to run their cotton farm.

She lost both of those sons, her youngest when he was twenty-two, the other when he was forty. I remember at five standing beside Daddy's grave with her and my mother. She was somber and silent, and I never heard her speak of either son again. In her day, you handled your grief privately, kept it locked away, picked up the pieces and went on.

Never having been ill, she had not been hospitalized until she broke her hip for the first time, at age seventy-nine. When the bone healed she got up and went on with her life.

By the time I came upon the scene to live in her house someone else did the housekeeping and cooking. Munnie sat in her rocker in front of a window and read or crocheted. Many beds were graced by her beautiful works of art.

I'd watch her needle fly and wonder what some of her thoughts might be. She was not a great talker, never complained, and during my teen years I didn't know how to draw her out so she might share her feelings. Mostly, I was awed by what other people referred to as a remarkable woman.

I wanted to ask things about my daddy, but somehow never had the courage, or knew how to proceed. She didn't die until I was twenty and married, but I still didn't know how to start a conversation about the past. In a way, her dignity was unapproachable. Not demonstrative by nature, she never hugged me or showed any outward affection after I left my young childhood.

Yet I knew she loved me and that I was important to her. Perhaps I even have some of her reserve and strength. I see the same iron mettle in my daughter, her great-granddaughter. And somehow, that is enough. I am grateful to have walked a short distance with her on her road to Emmaus and I would like to think I could follow in her footsteps of strength and fortitude.

Even though she didn't share her inmost concerns, I know she experienced her own dark nights of the soul. Because she was woman: daughter, and wife, and mother, I know she, too, had her time of watching black windows for dawn to come.

"Thank You, Father, for this tiny lady of another era who was blood of my blood, flesh of my flesh. I am grateful to have lived under her roof, and am proud I was her granddaughter. Her legacy lives on in me and in her great-grandchildren."

Chapter 16
A Family United

It was our son's tenth birthday. Since the children's father worked at night, we planned to have the birthday celebration on Saturday. Everything important had to wait for the weekend. Sometimes, I felt somewhat abandoned. It seemed the children and I were always alone, that our forces were scattered. Immediately I was ashamed of my unfair thought. My husband was working to supplement our farm income. He would have liked to have been with us.

Well, we couldn't just let the special day pass by unobserved! Brenda, our youngest who was recuperating from a tonsillectomy, suggested she and I fix an extra special supper for just the three of us.

Living on a farm meant we had to tend to the outside chores first. It was a beautiful winter evening, clear and still. The animals all fed, I decided it would be a good time to burn the paper trash.

We carried the trash cans outside and emptied them into the burner sitting in the field at the edge of the back yard. I struck a match to the paper and covered the top with the wire cover. It would be safe; there was not a stir of air. I could check it from the kitchen window while I prepared supper.

Wayne and his sister settled at the kitchen table doing homework. Brenda needed help with a problem so I sat down with them to see if we could figure it out together. That solved, I returned to my cooking efforts.

On the way to the range, I glanced out the window as I promised myself I would do. My heart skipped a beat. A whole fence of flames ran from the burning barrel out of sight behind the barn. "Dear God", I cried. "The field's on fire!"

I grabbed the phone to call the police who in return would call someone from the forestry unit at their home. It was all the fire protection our county offered rural residents at the time. Our only neighbor, some distance down the road, had no phone.

I told Brenda to stay inside and screamed for Wayne to come help me. It would be up to the two of us to keep the fire from spreading until help came. With poor weapons at that. Wayne had an old rake, and I had snatched up a burlap sack. Even if there had been time, I knew our little water hose wouldn't have made a dent.

Once outside, we could see the fire had not quite reached the barn. That's where we began to beat the flames out. The long barn housed all the farm equipment we owned. Adjoining it was the hangar that held my husband's single engine plane. With this in mind we stationed ourselves between the building and the conflagration.

Gradually we seemed to be succeeding in driving it back until I realized the higher stubble at the edge of the orchard had ignited. Quickly it spread with hungry flames leaping high over my head, as it spent its consuming energy in a race for our fruit trees. Precious trees, all that remained after the devastation of an earlier storm.

"Oh," I cried, "not our trees!" How could we handle this new threat? We were nearly exhausted. Both of us were winded, panting for breath, smudged black, our throats raw from the smoke. I knew if it caught the dried brush nearby, it would build force which could whip around and retrace its path to the barn, and maybe the house.

Was no one ever coming to help us? Other than the initial, "Dear God" plea, I had not had time to pray. I moaned now in desperation, "Lord, please help us. You can help us."

It was then I saw it. With the blaze roaring within inches of the first apple tree, help was supplied. I yelled at Wayne, "Bring the tin! We'll use the tin!"

My husband had straightened and piled long sheets of tin roofing in the field, tin ripped from our barn roofs by that earlier storm. My son brought them to me, and I threw them piece by jagged piece onto the flames.

We became a powerful team, that little boy and I. And we stamped out every threatening blaze! Through an instrument I ordinarily would not have chosen. For the nail-strewn tin, ripped and torn from the barn, was dangerous to pick up. Yet neither my son nor I had even so much as a scratch.

Later that night, the children in bed, I stood gazing across the charred field in the cold moonlight. It seemed unreal that a small boy and I had alone succeeded in such a monumental task.

Then I remembered Brenda had done her part by turning off the supper, and trying again to call for help which never responded. Knowing my daughter, I know she also encircled us with prayer.

And even though my husband had not been here to help us, he had prepared the tool we used. It is solid proof of what a family can do together. Why, our forces were not scattered at all! Even apart we were together. There is powerful strength in a family front united against any threat.

Suddenly it flooded over me that the exact moment I stopped depending solely on the strength of my young child and myself, help was supplied. Not only had God given me the idea of the tin, He aided us even further. While I did not actually see anyone, I know without any doubt we were not alone in the field on that terrifying night.

❦

"Through the wall of flames I could not see You, Lord, and I am not exactly sure how many Helpers You sent. I only know in that black spot on our Emmaus Road You were very present."

Chapter 17
The Lost Ones

As soon as I drove into the parking lot I noticed him. I could tell he was lost, but I decided to ignore it. I only had a minute or two to run into the store. Somebody else could help him!

But I couldn't keep my eyes off him. He seemed frantic in his haste, hurrying as fast as stiff legs would carry him from car to car. "Why do I always have to notice things like this?" I muttered to myself as I got out of the car, knowing full well I couldn't pass him by.

When I approached him, I recognized him as a respected elder in the nearby black community. Possibly I looked familiar to him too, for he seemed relieved when I quietly asked. "Have you lost your car?" Then confidentially I added, "I do that sometimes too."

He relaxed and said, "You do? Well, I sure have and I can't find my wife either."

Chatting comfortably as we slowly threaded our way through parked cars, it became a shared problem. He wasn't alone with his fear. The trouble was I didn't know his wife nor his car. My help was limited.

We soon came across a neighbor of his who knew the way to his car and his wife. I left him in the good hands of a friend, who not only could direct him to his goal but walked there with him. I had only played a small part.

Another day I was headed into town. I couldn't make out what it was, but up ahead something was lying in the street. The long line of traffic was moving too fast, especially since it had to swerve into the left lane to miss the object.

As I drew closer I could tell it was what I'd feared…Mercy was that a child lying beside it? "Lord, please make somebody stop and help them!"

By now I was nearly upon them. A young woman was kneeling in the street beside a fallen collie dog. "Oh, Lord," I began again, "Make somebody…."

About then the woman raised pleading eyes and looked right into my own. I was the help. I quickly pulled over and was out of the car before I knew it.

The woman cried, "Nobody would stop to help me! I can't move her myself." Together we slid the large dog out of the direct lane of traffic. I suggested a blanket to make a sling to transport her pet to her car. When she left I knelt in her place marveling at the love she had shown in order to protect her dog from further injury. The cars sped by, not even slowing. The dog looked at me calmly with trusting eyes.

When the owner returned with two neighbor ladies we all transferred the collie to the blanket, then to her car and on to the vet. Later I learned the beloved dog recovered.

Whenever I am prompted to pray, "Lord, make somebody…" I remember the young woman who raised pleading eyes to mine, and the elderly man with fear in his. It reminds me that if I pray for you it means I must be willing to stop and help you. Wherever you are, with whatever troubles you.

Enough like this has happened to me along my road of life to tell me there are certain times, places, and things which were meant for me to attend. What did Paul say? Some plant, some water. Some have my name on them, some are for others.

❧✦❧

"It is You, Lord, who has made me aware I must always be alert to Your lost ones. It was You who gave me the gift of seeing them. Not only are there helpers for me, You opened my eyes to see that I must also be a helper as well, on my road to Emmaus."

Chapter 18
I Asked God for Help and Got Cucumbers

My husband did not say, Go, hoe the cucumbers." He said, "The cucumbers need hoeing."

Fully aware of how much he had to do, and that this was something I could do, I was hoeing. But I wasn't liking it. My intentions may have started out well, but the more I hoed the angrier I became. I was muttering things such as, "One row would have been enough. Why did he plant so much of a useless product? There must be a half-acre!" (To be exact, there were six long rows.)

My temper and my hoeing accelerated to the same beat, along with my heart. I hoed faster, whacking up a cucumber here and there in retribution. Finally enough sanity swept in to tell me I might bring on a heart attack in the heat and that I should sit down. So I did, right between the rows, on a level where the plants eyed me like little green monsters.

An unhealthy combination of anger and self pity welled up inside and spilled over as tears ran down my face onto the ground, making tiny muddy droplets in the dirt. Actually, the cucumbers were only the scapegoats. My frustration was directed toward my husband and, in a deeper sense, toward God. I complained aloud, "What am I doing here, Lord? How can I be a field hand along with everything else? I asked you for help with my work, and you gave me cucumbers!"

My sniffling emotions and conversation with God in the morning stillness got the attention of our horse, who came close to the fence with little whickers of sympathy. "Yes, I know," I said to him. "I would have disciplined the children for such action."

The tears, nature's release, had washed out the anger. Now I was ashamed of my childish attitude. I wiped a smudgy hand across my cheek and thought, 'I'm no different from the Israelites who murmured against God in the wilderness.'

Chastened a bit, I got to my feet. A soft breeze rippled across my brow and stirred something inside as I looked across the acres I loved. I was not wandering around in the wilderness, which probably made my guilt worse. This *was* my promised land. And stewards of the land have a responsibility toward all of it.

It was true we didn't need all those cucumbers. However, I knew my husband's tendency toward over planting stemmed from the years we had farmed full time. I had loved and married a farmer. Even though his job had changed somewhat, the undercurrents of tilling the land ran deep. Besides, my marriage partner got a lot of pleasure from sharing our plenty. At that, another ugly fact reared its head, "It's my time he's so generous with, Lord. I want to be productive too, but I don't have time for me."

The ugliness vanished quickly this time, and I looked down at the plants again. Strangely, they were not menacing now; only healthy growth in the fertile soil. A thought crossed my mind, 'There must be something here for me to learn.'

I think God smiled then. Anyway, it seemed He said to me, "Look closely at the vines."

I had to get down again to do that, so I knelt in the soft earth and looked. My eyes were drawn first to the tiny yellow blooms, which are actually extensions of the cucumber itself. Between the stem and the bloom is the miniature product (provided, of course, it's a female blossom; the male bloom bears no fruit.)

I could see for myself: the fruit was already there. Given the proper growing conditions, nothing could stop them from full growth.

Without cultivation, however, little fruition will take place. Chopping out the weeds is a large part of cultivation. Which was what I was doing here in the first place. Apparently cucumbers were not all that needed cultivation.

I considered some of the weeds I needed to root out. The first was the harmful attitude I had toward my husband. If I corrected that, wouldn't it help my attitude toward God? While I resented some of the things required of me, in reality my husband had never asked anything of me that I couldn't handle. Neither had God.

Another weed was my wasted effort. If I had channeled all that angry energy into useful action, I could have completed the task by now. Performing any chore with fast, erratic movement wastes precious energy. I have watched field laborers hoe all day with less effort than I was exerting. They use a rhythmic motion which is evenly paced, making work more effective and easier as well.

Impatience is useless growth. I wanted things to happen my way. Right now, Lord! Skip the growing time; I didn't want to wait for it. Yet without it, my work will not grow to maturity. The fruit was already there. God had to get me down on my knees in a cucumber patch to see if for myself. I needed to accept God's timing instead of pushing for my own.

Possibly the wildest tangle in my private garden was self-fulfillment. I had certain ideas about what I wanted to do. I felt some of the byways I was forced to travel were a waste of me, as in the case of the hoeing. I was forgetting how the detours usually taught me something I would not have had a chance to learn otherwise. Experience had shown me that those times when self took a back seat and allowed Jesus His rightful place in the center of my life were the fullest, most completely right times.

I'm not rash enough to say that the next time I must work in the hot sun I shall approach it with enthusiastic fervor. But I shall not forget that when we ask God for help, He may surprise us with His answer. He will give us what we need, not what we think we need. And then He will permit us to see it was the best way, after all.

***

"It seems we have traveled a long way, Lord, from that day in the cucumber patch when You poured so many truths upon me. As I recall I had asked Your help then for more writing time. Instead You gave me the strangest answer, or so I thought. It was almost as if on that day, You took my hand and we ran down the Emmaus Road. Your answer came through the cucumbers themselves. I praise You."

***

Chapter 19
Light upon the Path

When my mother still lived in Ohio, I got a letter from her during a particularly difficult time in her experience. She related how she didn't know which way to turn. One sentence she wrote will forever stick in my mind. "I asked the Lord if He could show me light upon the path so I could see which way to go."

She went on to say He gave her the direction she needed. I don't remember the nature of the problem, but I realized she hit upon a gem of help in the request she made and wrote down. I have used it many times since.

In our walk along life's road we sometimes find ourselves in the dark, floundering along vainly in search of the right direction.

At thirteen I came to Georgia to live with my grandmother and aunt. School began with the usual pile of homework. The family who helped Uncle Bob and Aunt Berta run the dairy had twin girls in the same grade as me. Often we would do our lessons together either at my house or theirs.

On this night it was my turn to study at their house. A well defined path led through a long stretch of woods from one yard to the next. By the time we finished our studies and I started home it was pitch black outside. I never took a flashlight because the path was easily traversed if you began at the right entry into the woods. However, on that night somebody at their house turned off the porch light before I reached the starting place and I got off course at the beginning.

I was unaware I was headed in the wrong direction until I shuffled through thick leaves. The regular path was clean swept and much pressed down. I kept thinking instead of leaves and sticks I would soon feel smooth dirt under my bare feet. I expect I was walking in circles but at the time it just seemed to be taking much longer than usual getting home.

Suddenly, something sharply pricked the side of my ankle. I figured it was a thorn. Then when pain matched each step I took, I knew what had happened. Although I'd never been bitten by a snake, a thorn had never caused such pain.

I am certain God protects the young in special ways for I wasn't frightened. When I began to feel a bit woozy I remember saying aloud, "Please let somebody turn on the light." I kept straining to see a lighted window so I could aim toward it, but that side of our house was in darkness.

At last someone came into a room on the dark side and a light came on. From there I could walk toward the lighted window, and soon was calling out to Aunt Berta for help.

By then my foot was beginning to swell. Uncle Bob bundled me into the car and we went to town to the doctor's house. Dr. Ellis went into the kitchen and came back with what looked like a paring knife. He made an X at the fang's mark and suctioned the poison.

He and Uncle Bob determined that it had been a copperhead, the pit viper found in our section of the country. They sat and discussed current politics and worldly matters, giving time I suppose to see if I was going to keel over. If the doctor gave any kind of medication I do not remember it. I recall my foot and ankle stayed swollen for a few days and turned very dark.

It was only later that I became aware of how significant the experience was in relation to light upon the path. Over the years it has been to me a marvelous example of our Christian walk.

To begin with, I set off on the wrong path where everything was in darkness. In my wandering around a serpent attacked me. Some part of me knew I required light to escape from my dilemma. When I asked for it, light was provided. When I walked toward it I found safety.

I could easily relate to Mama's request of God to illuminate the way. Sometimes, the Emmaus Road is dark, but we only need to ask for the light to be given.

❦

"Even, Lord Jesus, when I travel a section of the road without human companionship and darkness overcomes me, I know from very personal experience that Mama was right. When I ask, You will illumine the pathway ahead, for You alone are the true Light."

Chapter 20
Paula Is with Me

Very early in my walk with the Lord Jesus, when I would hear someone say, "God said this or that to me," I might look interested and respond politely, while privately I thought they had a wild imagination. Or they had a high opinion of themselves. I wasn't having any across the table discussions with God. Why were they any different?

Not that I didn't talk to God, but I believed He "speaks to us" through His Holy Word. Which I have found to be very true. It was farther on in my walk I learned He also communicates with us more personally, if the lines are open.

In John's Gospel we are told that "God is a Spirit; and they that worship Him must worship Him in spirit and in truth" (John 4:24 KJV). His Spirit speaks to our spirit. When I prayed, that's the way I always envisioned Him, as a Spirit. It changed one day when the humanity of Jesus Himself spoke to me. Never before and never since have I experienced the Presence of an unseen physical entity as strongly as I did on a day when He walked with me out of the woods and onto the path which led across the field to our house.

Feeling the need for a quiet time on that late afternoon, I left our daughter, ill with mononucleosis, in bed to rest. I went to a favorite spot in the woods on our farm to pray. Brenda was not the only one for whom I meant to intercede.

Brenda and Paula had been classmates and friends since first grade. Now they were fifteen and it was almost Christmas. Brenda's illness was not life threatening. Paula, after surgery to replace a shunt in her head, was in a coma in an Atlanta hospital.

Paula, a popular child, was the kind who drew people to her. She was smart, had a loving, wonderful family, and everything going for her. Of course, Paula was going to wake up and come out of the strange sleep she was in! How could it be otherwise? Weren't we all praying for her?

There, with the trees towering over me, on the ridge above the swamp I prayed for Brenda's recovery. And then I poured my heart out for Paula and for her family sitting around the silent hospital bed. I asked for her healing, that even at this moment God would open her eyes and she would speak to her loved ones.

When I finished interceding I felt no special response. No assurance such as I often sensed after prayer. Doubt began to close in. Did God even hear? This very day I wanted Paula to wake up! I wanted her family to be happy again.

Dejected, I retraced my steps. Just as I reached the path at woods end and started up the rise across the field, I sensed I was not alone. Someone was with me. Startled I spun around to see who, when suddenly I knew. The truth swept over me so strongly I could feel the rough texture of the brown robe which Jesus wore. I could actually "see" its color.

My eyes did not see a physical body, but the Presence was so powerful that my mind saw exactly what I have just written. The robe was brown and rough textured. I remember wondering how I knew that. But I did know.

Warmth, and comfort, and gentleness surrounded me and He

spoke very clearly to my mind, "Paula is all right. Paula is with me." That's all. I finally was able to continue walking home. I didn't know what it meant; was she to be healed? He didn't say that, only that she was with Him. Was she already gone?

As soon as I reached the house a phone call let me know she was still alive. What was it all about, and why was I given such a message when Paula's family needed it? I wasn't even what you would call a personal friend.

I didn't have any answers, although I did not doubt what I had heard. The next day a friend called to tell us Paula had just died. An interval of hours after I received the words, "Paula is with me."

I have asked the question a thousand times: where are those who are in comas? Was she indeed with our Lord during that deep sleep even before her physical body shut down forever?

To this day I have no concrete answer. I shared the experience only with Brenda. Somehow it didn't seem fitting to tell Paula's family. After all, my child had recovered.

As time passed, every once in a while I would question why I was granted this knowledge. But I never doubted its reality. I remember it as vividly today as when it occurred on that cold December afternoon.

It was several years before I was impressed to write about it. Now was the time to tell them. I wrote a letter to her parents, still experiencing hesitation as how it might bring a return of their raw grief. I explained I would like to use it in something I was writing.

I didn't have to wait long. A prompt reply came and in it they graciously gave me permission to tell of the experience. Her father wrote that he had been unable to find peace about his daughter's death until my letter, and somehow it had given him that.

In reality my faith was greatly lacking. After I prayed for

Paula's healing I remember the doubt I experienced before I received that wonderful revelation. Even with the doubt though I was listening with every ounce of my being for more. Perhaps it was the reason I was given the precious news about their beloved child. Now, however, I knew it was more.

I wasn't supposed to share it until this point in their lives. Now was the moment, the time they needed to hear what our Lord Jesus had given me on the day He held Paula in His arms to be with Him.

This special encounter reinforced some of what I had been gathering all along. As I advanced beyond the "milk" stage spiritually, I became aware that God does speak to us through the impressions and actual words we can hear in our minds and with our hearts.

If a certain impression or command comes to me several times, I have learned it is time to stop and listen. I wish I could say every time I need an answer I get it. Often I struggle with making the right decisions, and on occasion make explicitly wrong ones.

To receive, one thing is definitely essential—we have to keep our receivers in order. Our petitions must be that which can be in His will, and our praises have to be sincere.

If we have any doubt as to the validity of what we are receiving, we can check it out against His teachings in the Bible, which is His revelation to us. He will never direct us to anything contrary to His teachings. We really don't have to muddle along alone. His gift was that the Holy Spirit would teach us, comfort, and guide us.

I am convinced if God gives us a special message, He will help us remember. And He will let us know when His time is right for us to share it.

"Lord Jesus, You called yourself the Son of Man. We speak of Your humanity, yet we fail to fully understand. The greatest mission of the Holy Spirit is to magnify the reality of Your Person, the very real Person of You, Lord Jesus, who walks beside us down our Emmaus Roads."

Chapter 21
Who Am I Really?

We were decorating our Christmas tree when something awoke and began flying around. A grasshopper had chosen the sanctuary of the cedar to rest until the frigid temperatures claimed him. The tree protected him so well the warm room was able to bring about his complete resuscitation. I couldn't toss him out in the ten-degree weather, so I plopped him into an old terrarium in the basement, and named him Lazarus.

When our son came home from college, I showed him my treasure. He said quite bluntly, "Well, Mom, you can't lay this one on us. He's all yours."

He referred to all the rescued creatures we had stowed away in substitute homes throughout his and his sister's growing years. Such items were categorized The Children's Collection. But now, it was down to the bare bones of honest acknowledgment. Truthfully, it was me who did a lot of the rescuing. For some reason I felt it was equated with immaturity; it sounded more acceptable to blame it on the children.

Wayne had handed me a key to a new door of opportunity. If not for him and the grasshopper, I might never have discovered what freedom lay in individuality. It was my first inkling I may have frittered away fruitful years doing what was expected, heedless of an inner disquiet that might have been God trying to reach me in a still, small voice.

The dissatisfaction became louder when I reached forty, synonymous somehow with having climbed to the top of a high hill. My babies had become toddlers, then school children, then teenagers and now they were grown. Previous patterns of acceptability as a proper mother seemed to fit nowhere. I wasn't needed in the same way as before. Wandering around in a middle-age trauma, I had to decide where to go from here.

Should I join a dedicated group and conform to post-forty endeavors, whatever they might be? A stereotyped version of accepted lifestyle didn't interest me a bit. Were all my previous involvements based on nothing stronger than a frazzled belief in doing "what I was supposed to do?" What percentage of my present activities were motivated by what was expected of me against what I longed to do? Or far more important what God wanted me to do.

The decision confronting me: did I have enough courage to throw away supports of popularity and approval? It would mean I was not at the beck and call of anyone and everyone who decided what my purpose in life might be.

It was necessary to lay it all before God. What did He want me to weed out, and what to cultivate? To improve characteristics that made me who I am, I set forth to reclaim some of the dreams God had given me and I had set aside.

Our original differences are our Creator's gift to us. We are not carbon copies. Talents, interests, dreams, hopes are not inborn to give us misery, but to direct us to our best self, and in turn our best service to our Maker.

As I wavered on that fortyish hilltop I was given a protracted view which lasted long enough for me to discover I had been hiding behind a substitute front. This was not the total me. There was something else I was meant to do. Here was a whole new chance for another charge at that hill.

That's when God gave me the courage to not only "write it down" but to begin to share with others what He led me to write.

Lazarus, the grasshopper, lived until spring. By then it was warm enough to place him on a warm tree limb in the orchard where he peacefully breathed his last fresh air. I know well the damage his kind can do to gardens and such, but this particular one had resurrected in me a new understanding of who I am. Through him the truth had set me free. I felt I owed the same to him.

❦

"Only You, Lord, in Your greatness, and goodness, and with a precious sense of humor could teach me to open my eyes through yet another of Your creations. Thank You for helping me find more of myself and Your purpose for me, that it might be used to aid someone else in their discovery. It's a true relief to discover we are not all meant to be the same."

Chapter 22
The Blue Damson Plum

Every year when spring turns the corner and the world is freshly abloom, our family remembers the plum tree and how a tiny miracle occurred when from an ancient root a sprout appeared. Only a few blossoms heralded its activity, yet it bore fruit. With a tenacity beyond our understanding the tenacious little tree held on past its normal span. Later it would supply a special need at a specific time.

I had noticed the new growth in April and said to my husband, "Next time I see Uncle Charlie, I'll tell him it looks as if we have a Blue Damson plum blooming."

We didn't know why it was important to him. Only that he had spent a portion of the summer before unsuccessfully searching for a remnant of those trees cultivated here when he was a young man in his father's house.

I never got around to telling him about the bush I had seen in bloom. That July in his eighty-fourth year he became very ill.

Uncle Charlie always had such a good relationship with life that even then he was making preparation for another spring. As I sat beside his bed, he spoke of things needing attention: the pasture limed, the scuppernong vine pruned, the roof over the south bedroom repaired. He told me where the roofing was stored, assuming that some of our generation would take care of it. I half listened, nodding when it seemed proper, preoccupied with shock that the strength of this amazing old man, great-uncle to my husband, was spent.

When I realized what he was implying, self-will thrust it away with a repulsive shove. I refused to think about it. He wasn't going to die! I wouldn't let him. He was our last tie with two generations removed, and my need to lean was great.

No matter how I tried though, I couldn't escape the thought that for him another season might not come. It hung thick and heavy like the oppressive air of the hot summer day.

I tried to fasten my thoughts upon the good things. Indeed, special comfort came from knowing he had enjoyed excellent physical health, and an active, fruitful life. Nor did I worry about his spiritual well-being, for he had shared with me that Jesus had been his personal Friend for more years than I had lived.

Still I wasn't ready to let him go. Fierce in my determination to push the fear away, I meant to hold back time.

As the days wore on, I became more involved with caring for his physical needs. He took memory trips into the past. How happy he was that we had chosen to live in the original home place down the road. He recalled visits with gifts of fresh-churned butter, and johnny cakes, or peppermint sticks for the children. If we weren't home, he would leave his treats and write messages for us in the firm earth close to the back steps.

One afternoon as his memory meandered in and out of past and present, my mind made sashays down its own channels. How I'd like to do something special for him! A gift. Something that would change the whole pattern of the summer, and he would be well again.

I was brought out of my reverie by what he was saying, "Funny that I couldn't find a trace of those plums. We had so many; I can still taste the jelly Mother used to make."

Of course! The Blue Damson. But I didn't know if those early blooms had been productive. If they had, wouldn't they be gone? Besides, such a small thing, I thought. It's silly to bother. It was then a gentle urge whispered, "Why don't you go see?"

I hurried home. Before I reached the tree, I could see plums scattered around its branches. With those added to what I found on the ground, I decided to make preserves.

I worked over them, willing them to turn out well. Done in time for supper, they had produced only a half pint. Uncle Charlie sat up and ate his fill with warm biscuits and butter, the first genuine enjoyment he'd shown in days. My gift had been well chosen.

When I told him about the small crop, his blue eyes twinkled as he chuckled and said, "Well, it was just enough. Things have a way of turning out what we need when we need them."

Suddenly I understood why the familiar plums were important to him. It wasn't food he sought. It was a brief return to carefree days of youth. His need had arisen out of a yearning for his older generation. The plum was only a symbol of irrevocable ties to loved ones. Nothing, not even death, can break that silver cord of love. I held the knowledge close to me. Just knowing helped me through what turned out to be Uncle Charlie's last summer.

Never again on our farm did we find a Blue Damson. More strangely, the growth that had appeared was brittle and dead by the next season. It's almost eerie the way it happened, until we remember life is like that. Uncle Charlie was right. Often it doesn't take much to answer a need, or to satisfy and comfort a yearning of the heart.

Only God can take the seemingly insignificant and in his own way and time fill some special purpose.

❧❀❦

"For this gentle man I thank You, Lord, that with him and me You walked our Emmaus Road, where You met our needs along the way. And for him, the final way with the plum tree."

❧❀❦

The chapter "Uncle Charlie and the Blue Damson Plum" minus the prayer was originally published in *Home Life* magazine, April 1983. Also in *Catholic Digest,* August 1983.

Chapter 23
Coloring Books and Crayons

As my husband opened his present from Reba and Nelson, my eye was caught by the expression on Nelson's face. The room fairly lit up with his smile. I was familiar with that smile. It had lighted up my childhood.

We were celebrating no special occasion, unless you considered our annual visit to Ohio an occasion. But then, in Nelson's book you didn't need a reason to give a gift.

When Nannie and Granddaddy found my mother in the orphanage and took her home they had one daughter, Reba, who was seven. Mama was one year older. The girls grew up together and when Mama married it wasn't long before Reba was wed to Nelson. After my daddy died when I was five, Nelson was another male figure in the family whom I looked up to, although I was shy with him.

He was partially deaf which made it difficult for communication. He was a good father to Clarene and Helen and later to his only son, Jerry, but I can't ever remember seeing him hug them. Reserved perhaps because of his deafness, he seemed a little unapproachable.

At one time we all lived in Nannie and Granddaddy's house. It was during the depression when there was barely enough money for essentials. Nelson was lucky to have a job and he worked hard for his family. Sometimes on payday he would bring his children crayons and color books, or some other small delight.

I remember the color books best because they were my favorites. For he never, ever left me out. I would hang back thinking maybe this time it was only for Clarene and Helen, and then he would beckon me to come for mine too.

After I grew up, Edwin and I hoped we might somehow repay the favors. My husband and Nelson had hit it off well. In fact, I never before heard Nelson talk and laugh as much as he did with Edwin. But it always seemed that Nelson and Reba were the ones who were still doing thoughtful things for us. In my family Reba was the main one who expressed great pride in my writing aspirations giving me encouraging boosts now and then.

It came to me as I watched Edwin open his gift that Nelson's return was in the giving. He received joy from simple gestures that could not be paid back. It's the inner warmth which comes from having shared a part of yourself. It's happiness and joy all mingled together until a glow is turned on somewhere inside your soul.

As I said, I saw Nelson as an undemonstrative person. Years later on our last visit to his house when he was very ill, he stood outside the door and clasped my hand in his as we said goodbye. Every year when we would leave he seemed sad at our going but would brighten up and say, "Well, I'll see you again next year."

This time was different. He said, "Well, I'll see you," and he paused…and finished with, "Somewhere." Never a man of many words, his pause spoke volumes to me. For he had made a profession of faith in our Lord Jesus a few years before. I knew he referred to eternity, and he had the hope we would meet again. I have accepted that I can never repay him for coloring books, and crayons, and other kindnesses. Except to pass it on to someone else and make their average day extra special like Nelson did for me so many times.

"My cup overflows, Lord Jesus, when I think of all those who shared my childhood journey down Emmaus. No one could ever take my daddy's place, but You always sent someone when there was a need or a longing. How can I ever thank You or them?"

Chapter 24
Burden Bearers

The sudden impact of an emergency can shake the foundation of even the strongest. As I look back it seems to me that my husband spent a good segment of his life scaring me half to death. Not purposefully. Through accident or illness his life was thrown into jeopardy on several occasions.

On that fall morning he had gone to the woods to cut firewood. I usually didn't join him until he had the tree cut in proper lengths for splitting. Then together we would use the log splitter to prepare the wood for our heater.

I hurried around getting house work done before my help was required. Suddenly, from the bedroom I saw him pass by the window. Why was he back so early? One look and I knew something was dreadfully wrong.

As I helped him inside and into a chair, he gasped out that he wanted to get a shower so I could take him to the emergency room. I ignored such a request and called 911.

While we waited the few minutes it took for the paramedics to arrive I learned what occurred. When he tipped one of the outer limbs of a felled tree with the chain saw to free it from where it had caught, the tree whirled and threw him through the air about fifty feet. The tree had hung on vines he didn't see and the pressure released by his cut caused the reaction that nearly cost Edwin his life.

The ambulance had come, the paramedics had put him in the trauma suit, and rushed him off to the hospital. The adrenalin rush which comes when we are under great stress had gotten me through the moments of getting the necessary medical aid. I had driven myself to the hospital.

Now my husband was in emergency and I was more frightened than I had ever been in my life. Until I knew something definite I had not called anyone but my daughter. It would take her a couple of hours to join me.

Waiting, I felt completely crushed by the burden. Fear spread over me in great pulsing rushes. Then, I looked up and ambling down the hall was my husband's only brother.

Robert was at the hospital for another reason with no inkling that his brother was battling for his life. He was as astonished to see me as I was him. Seldom have I been so glad to see someone. This was family! Somebody familiar. I wasted no time in transferring part of my burden to him, and he, bless him, lost no time in picking it up.

In those first panicky hours and in the days of my husband's recuperation Robert and Helen and their daughter, Joy, were towers of strength and comfort. Family! Nobody can support you in quite the same way as family.

Years later when Edwin was undergoing more cancer surgery, the oncology surgeon was explaining to me that he was unable to extract all the growth because of its position behind the carotid artery. Robert was present as well, again helping me bear a burden I felt would smother me. Helen had been with me during the surgery prior to that. In times such as this when great weights were cast upon me, they and our niece Joy held a great part of it up.

Although I knew about sharing burdens, never had the experience been as meaningful as it was the day Robert came sauntering down that hospital corridor.

The simple act of conveying to him what had happened, of sharing the load, lightened it to bearable levels. I marvel how God strengthens us, and how at precise moments He sends us burden-bearers to help us carry these pressing weights we all must face from time to time.

❧✺❧

"Lord, even to this day my heart fills with gratitude to Helen, Robert, Joy, and to You, Lord, who sent them. Your word has said when we bear one another's burdens, we fulfill Your law. Bless those especially who along this road have born part of my burdens, to enable me to carry them."

Chapter 25
It's How You Set Your Sights

My husband's mother suffered a heart attack. We were allowed fifteen minute visits every two hours. The family felt the support of loved ones would be an aid in Mama Pearl's recovery so we set certain times for one of us to be there.

It was my first exposure to a Cardiac Care Unit. I stood in the middle of the room trying not to look at the EKG monitor, nor notice the pulse rate flashing continually. It gave me chills to think those funny, bumpy lines could straighten out like I'd seen them do on television.

Heavily sedated, she slept. Her body lay thin and inert under the sheet. Her face looked pinched and colorless. I moved quietly, knowing rest was essential. A bit fearfully I allowed my eyes to travel around the room, and back to all the tubes and wires fastened to her and leading to the mechanical watchdogs which filled the entire wall at the head of her bed. I noted the oxygen tubes, the IV dripping sustaining fluid into her weakened system, and thought how quickly the human body can change from ambulatory independence to a stricken vessel.

Aware I was getting bogged down in negative thought, I tried

CLARA WALLACE NAIL

to pray for her recovery. Mama Pearl had an unusually positive personality. No long face for her. She was always ready with a laugh or a joking retort. Had she been awake she might, in fact, have said to me. "For goodness sake, I'm not dead until the Lord is ready for me. Think something happy!"

Right there in her room, I tried to establish in my mind a picture of better health. I worked at it all the way home, but I didn't have much success, nor at praying. All I could see were those tubes and wires.

Then suddenly a silly scene came into my mind. I laughed, and veered my thoughts to other channels but it always came back to one particular incident. I didn't understand why, but I tuned it in and began to concentrate on the memory.

The incident occurred one summer when the children were small. Mama Pearl and I were in the orchard behind the barn gathering the last of the meager supply of apples the trees produced that year. We endeavored to get every last one. With unswerving determination we shook the trees, punched them with sticks, threw rocks into the branches. High on the topmost branch of the last tree clustered on one stem were three huge, absolutely perfect specimens which we were unable to dislodge.

It was then I went to the house for the .22 rifle. I am not a hunter, but in our family we learned to shoot. In rural areas of that time you never knew when you might have to protect yourself or your farm animals from a predator.

When I returned with the gun, my mother-in-law's expression of doubt plainly revealed her lack of faith in my ability to bring down those apples. With her face raised to the sun, I could see her laughing as I raised the rifle, carefully setting the sights not too low, nor too high, but right on the tiny twig which held the apples so tightly.

Steady, my aim directly on target, I squeezed the trigger. The bullet clipped the twig right behind the apples, which plummeted to the soft grass below. It was my turn to laugh when she yelped, "Wow! where's me a wagon wheel?" I knew what she meant. In TV westerns the cowboys would sometimes jump behind a wagon wheel for protection during shootouts.

After that, every time the dour hospital scene came to mind, God switched me over to the vision of a happier day.

I wouldn't have believed it, but exactly two months later we were walking together in the orchard again. In the sun and laughing. It was then I remembered what else she said that day we gathered the apples.

She said, "Well! I didn't think you could do it. But you thought you could. I guess that's what did it, wasn't it? When you took aim, you believed you could do it."

She was right. I never for one minute doubted that if I lined up the sights just so I could clip the twig. Down deep inside myself I knew I would not miss. I remember the exultant sensation of knowing I would cut the twig exactly where I aimed. That was what God wanted me to remember. When I lined up the sights with complete confidence, not too low, nor too high, not to the left, nor the right, to a picture of Mama Pearl laughing in the sun, I claimed the proper target. Even when I couldn't pray with words, my mind held the vision.

"Thank You for Mama Pearl, Lord, and for her years with us after that first attack. She was my friend as well as a good mother-in-law. It would have been much harder to raise the children without her. For a long trek down the Emmaus Road she helped me, never criticized, taught me many things, shared an empathy. I miss her greatly although I am glad You took her before her son, my husband, had to leave. That would have caused her such pain."

Chapter 26
Deep Down I Knew

After the experience when Mama Pearl was in the hospital and I was caused to remember the incident of the apples in the orchard, I felt there was more here that I needed to unravel. More God wanted me to understand.

For example, how did I know I would hit the target I aimed for? I thought about it a lot. It was not an audacious, superior feeling. It was more like pure confidence smoothly flowing, coming from within me yet empowered by something beyond my meager self.

This was not my first encounter with that power. Back in the spring of 1953 somehow I knew by that time next year, I would be a mother. When I used to sit and wait for Edwin in the car when he came to see about farm matters here on our farm, somehow I knew I would one day live in this very old house of my husband's great-grandparents. One certain year when I entered a writer's contest and mailed it off, somehow I knew deep inside that my article would be successful. And so on.

Is much more available to us than we use? What about being overly confident? Does it then become presumption? It may be

THEN MY EYES WERE OPENED

hard to separate our audacity from this peculiar knowledge that this power is in us, or could come from within us.

The Scripture says, "Faith is the substance of things hoped for, the evidence of things not seen." I mulled this over for a while and prayed, "Help me figure this out, Lord" (Hebrews 11:1 KJV).

While I mulled, a memory asserted itself. I was on my way to town on an errand and just as I crossed the creek a strange sight met me. It was a beagle sort of dog in big trouble. I parked beside the ditch and waited.

She came to me in lumbering fashion, weaving her head from side to side. It was as if she knew she was to come to me, and I knew she was to come to me for help. She had the broken ring of a glass jug hung around her neck. Apparently she had stuck her head in the big jar to lick whatever had been in it and then charged around until she shattered the jar, leaving herself trapped in the jagged circle.

She had no fear of me as I leaned over and grasped the ring in my hands. She gave a little pull and was free. With a look of gratitude she turned and continued on her way. I got in the car and went on to town.

It was like we had an appointment, no big deal, just do your part and move on. The answer came: it's an appointment of what is meant to be. It's setting our sights precisely on whatever target is ahead, and knowing with certainty that we will not miss. Success comes from unblocked inner knowledge. Because if we are appointed to do it, God will have unblocked the way and unleashed the power.

It's the substance and evidence of what we cannot see, but deep inside faith is the eye that sees the target. It's not audacity after all. It is simply getting ourselves out of the way so God can open the channels to belief.

"I praise You, Lord, for the targets and appointments you make along the road as You journey beside me. How can I miss?"

Chapter 27
Change of Plans

Although I had experienced God's intervention before in the course of daily living, it had never come to me quite so persistently as it did on a particular morning when Lena was in trouble.

I awoke early with an indefinable pull toward something I must do, like on the days you awake with big plans mapped out. I lay quietly getting my bearings, mentally listing the day's schedule, willing my foggy mind to latch onto the reason for its search.

Then, it fastened upon Lena, but I quickly discarded the notion. It was decided yesterday that she would not need me today.

Long before we were here, Lena had lived at the end of our road. Soon after we moved into Great-grandfather Nail's house, Lena came to pay a neighborly visit. From that time on she helped me over many bumps in my daily walk. She didn't mind one bit telling me when I was wrong about something, especially if she felt I was remiss in my wifely or motherly duties.

Childless herself, she took care of others. My children were intrigued by her. Wayne, our eldest, thought she was wonderful. As long as she lived she kept on her wall a collage he made for her when he was five.

Elderly, alone, and now ill, she reached a point where she was unable to care for her total needs. It was my turn to help her. Yesterday, though, she said she could manage the next day with the food I had taken her. Knowing how busy I was with young children and farm chores, she assured me, "I'll be all right; you been lettin' things at home pack up. Everything I need is right here."

I realized she wished to be as little trouble as possible and decided to obey her order. All her life, Lena had been the helper, waiting on others. Her generation called it "in the service", and although she and I had a special friendship, I knew when to allow her to keep the dignity of the position she chose. She was never my servant; our relationship had always been friend and neighbor, and I usually took her advice for her experience far surpassed my own.

For that reason I tried to ignore the inner prompting urging me to go see about her. All during the morning preparation getting my family ready for their day, the persistent worry would not leave me. It buzzed inside my head like a worrisome bee. I loaded the washer, and put the dishes in the sink to soak. But the nagging wouldn't let me alone.

I even argued with myself, and the inner voice which prodded me to disregard yesterday's plan. I listed the excuses Lena herself gave me. "She doesn't need me; she told me to stay home!"

Suddenly resolves and excuses were cast aside and I headed down the road. Once on her porch, I called her name. Up to now she had been able to let me in, but this time she didn't appear. I heard a slight sound inside and when I tried the knob it turned at my touch.

I found her weakened and sick on the sofa in her living room, close to the ancient coal heater that fell short of heating her small house. On the floor in front of the heater lay a smoldering mound of old quilts, clothes, rags, anything she could reach from where she lay. The broken hinge on the stove door had given way and live coals had fallen onto the floor.

Too weak to get up and tend it properly, she had done the next best thing. The only way she could control the blaze was to systematically add another layer of cloth. While it didn't extinguish the smolder, it smothered its full burst. Now her weapon had given out, and tiny flames were beginning to lick through the center of the mound.

After I removed the charred remains and cleaned up the floor, I turned my attention to her. Horrified, I asked what had probably been on her own mind, "What on earth were you going to do when the clothes gave out?"

Feebly, she replied, "I prayed, so I knew you'd come."

God had not failed her faith which I knew to be strong, and He used me even though I tried to tune the summons out.

Many times I have pondered her words, "I prayed; I knew you'd come." Since that day when God changed my schedule and led me to my friend, I am more alert to a persistent summons, the kind that does not diminish but increases in urgency. Now I know that someone's life may depend on my response.

And I am reminded how wondrously God can bring us together when we human beings need each other.

❦

"How close you are, Lord, when I listen to Your inner voice! We both know how special Lena was with her great faith in You. I am honored to have been her friend in the years that spanned our walk toward Emmaus."

Chapter 28
When the Martins Return

Certain changes occur which become shifting points in our lives, and nothing is ever the same afterward. On the afternoon I received word that my only aunt had been taken to the hospital after an automobile accident, I instinctively knew this was one of them.

Aunt Berta, the last member of my father's family, at eighty-nine was still a fiery bundle of determination and independence. A solid rock in my life, she had always been there for me and I couldn't imagine life without her. Yet without warning I was thrust into a position of decision making concerning her life and her affairs.

Our normal pattern of daily existence came to a standstill. During the weeks of her hospitalization, I practically knocked myself out trying to keep my household in as efficient order as possible. At best it consisted of a swipe here and there. In every way physically, emotionally, and spiritually, I was defeated and exhausted. Plus, my heart was breaking. It hurt desperately to see her injured and sick, looking so vulnerable and old.

My good friend Catherine advised, "Put everything else on a

back burner; that's the only way you can handle crisis such as this." She was right. No matter how much I tried to keep the home routine humming, I barely touched the surface. Aunt Berta, who needed me more than anybody else, was top priority right now. The rest would have to adjust to that.

I was grateful that part of the time she was lucid enough to share in decisions concerning her welfare. Her premise had always been—"*Something* must take us out of this world." Quite prepared to accept this as her way out, she had repeatedly asked to go home in order to be in familiar surroundings as she took her leave.

She had no wish to be kept alive mechanically. When her time came I was to relinquish her, and allow no lifesaving heroics. It was necessary for me to settle that within myself.

However, it wasn't simply a matter of taking an ailing patient home from the hospital. Not only was the immediate problem of her heart now involved, our major fear was the serious damage the accident had done to her throat. It necessitated that everyone who would be with her learn how to use a suction machine designed to clear the throat of mucus buildup. My greatest horror was that she would choke to death. The experiences of her nearly strangling in the hospital were bad enough. To imagine dealing with it at home was unsettling, to say the least.

Added to the anguish and grief I felt at losing her, I had to contend with those who thought it crazy to attempt caring for her at home. But the hospital had done all they could do and were now urging me to make other arrangements.

With too much money to qualify for government aid and too little to see my way clear for round the clock nursing, I had reached the end of the line with no idea what to do. And, it seemed, no one to turn to.

I came home for a few hours with the decision facing me on

the morrow. I had come to the place my beloved Aunt Berta had prepared me for my entire life. I'd never felt more alone nor more desperate. The walls of the house pressed in on me. I put on my coat and took the dogs outside on that cold December evening.

A beautiful night, it was bright as dawn with a full moon in a clear, silent sky. The external appearance of peace was in sharp contrast to my inner discord. Frightened, uncertain, I carried the burden of making this decision totally alone. While input from others had been given, the final say was mine. How on earth was I to manage what seemed insurmountable problems?

Such was the setting when I began to pray, the words tumbling out in an agonized flood. Immediately after this emptying a line of Scripture came to my mind, "I will lift up mine eyes unto the hills from whence cometh my help" (Psalms 121:1 KJV). No distant hills were visible so I looked up into the heavens, and there in full view of my focus, silhouetted against the moonlit sky, stood the martin pole.

Usually in the winter months whenever I look at the martin gourds, their silence gives me a sad, lonely feeling. The purple martins are such busy creatures during the spring and summer they spend with us, I miss their cheerful chatter when they leave.

Now, looking upward into the cold winter sky, peace like a warm cloak began to enfold me, and suddenly I was not alone. A very definite Presence was with me, calming me into a listening stillness with an ordinary familiar object.

My tears stopped, my confusion and hopelessness vanished. Then God's Presence through His Holy Spirit clearly gave me this promise,—"As surely as in past seasons you have witnessed the joyful return of the purple martins, so will there be a return to a more peaceful time. By the time the martins return, this difficulty and heartbreak will pass. Trust me and I will show you."

After that things began to change. Where before I had met all sorts of obstacles as to the proper course to take, affairs began to fall into place. Doors previously closed, opened when I approached them. People, equipment, finances—an undertaking of immense proportions, singularly the most difficult task I had ever organized or faced—all came together.

We were home! And we were prepared to give her the care she required. I had fulfilled Aunt Berta's last request of me. Later, when she was granted the dignity of leaving this world in a peaceful sleep from the sanctity of the house where she had lived her lifetime, I experienced the sorrow of loss but not of regret.

The following February I sat in the warm sun at the foot of the martin pole cleaning out the gourd houses my husband had handed down. He was busy replacing those I had finished. It was a routine, tranquil time. Suddenly a familiar sound caught my attention. I gazed upward and there perched on the crosspiece above my husband's head was the first martin scout. Home again from his long journey, he greeted us with cheerful chirps and chatters. Just the same as every year before!

The martins had returned, exactly as God had promised me that winter night. Some things do not change and their very constancy gives us stability to cling to.

It occurred to me then that something else happened the night of His promise. Not only did God meet me at my basic need, He gave me something extra. Where I kept seeing my aunt old and ill, after the night at the martin pole I saw her as she was when I was a little girl, the most beautiful aunt in the whole world, young, vitally alive, pretty, and petite.

A strange little incident, yet it carried me through the stressful time of her leave-taking with a strength I didn't know I possessed. And in my inner vision she is still wrapped in an aura of springtime.

❦

"Lord Jesus, that beautiful night You met me at the martin pole is such a special memory. At that point on Emmaus, You infused me with Your promise and new strength. You understood Aunt Berta's great longing to go home and take her leave from that house as her mama and papa had done, and Harrell, the brother she so deeply loved. You helped me be the instrument who answered her longing. I praise You."

Chapter 29
Miss Berta

In the southern part of our United States the term Miss placed before a lady's given name has long been used as a title of respect. We are seeing a new age with different cultural influences change that practice, but it was a pleasant manner of treating women out of their teens with regard, especially those of more mature years.

As time marches on many of these older ones are forgotten. Their term of distinction has swept past us in the pages of history turned beyond their remembrance.

Once the name, "Miss Berta", was known by all McDonough residents because she was present on the main street in town as the only telegraph operator. During a period when her contemporaries were mostly stay-at-home housewives and mothers, my Aunt Berta was making a local name for herself in the workforce.

Her Telegraph Office sign hangs on my kitchen wall. It reads, "Week Days - 8 a.m. to 7 p.m. Closed 11:30-12:30, 5 - 6, lunch and dinner. Sundays and holidays, 9 - 10 a.m. and 5 - 6 p.m." (And we complain about long work days!)

Like anything Aunt Berta set out to do, she did this job with dedication and commitment and, I am certain, with great compassion. For people who lived in the country a telegram was a sobering experience for it often carried bad news such as the death of a loved one. Miss Berta, I am told, would do whatever it took to get what came through on her wire to the recipient. It gave her joy when she could deliver good news.

I can still smell her office, and hear the click of her key as she sent or received messages. Even now, I hold the key in my hand and wonder how many missives were sent and received with it, and how the messages affected those who waited for the words that came in the dots and dashes of Morse code.

During the 30's I lived in Ohio. I was the only child around who got a telegram from Santa Claus, no less, on Christmas Eve! In it he always admonished me to be good and to be sure to convey the same word to Clarene and Helen. Years later, of course, it was easy to figure out who was responsible for those greetings…further proof of her love for family and spreading of good cheer.

After Aunt Berta's funeral, Edna Evans Hammock wrote a piece for the county paper that I am quoting below. It tells better than I can what some of those messages meant to those who waited, and what part Miss Berta played in each one as she manned her daily post.

Edna called her article, "Remembering 'Miss Berta'" and this is what she wrote:

> Not much has been said of Mrs. Berta Payne since her passing, but then not much was said before, except to marvel at her agility and determination for that was the way she wanted it, for she was a very independent and unassuming little lady.
>
> Sometimes, I would meet her in the grocery store,

THEN MY EYES WERE OPENED

prior to her death, but her hearing was such that I could not make her understand all I wanted to say, so I would like for this to be said to the ones she left behind, that might not know.

My fondest memories of Ms. Berta was when she was telegraph operator in McDonough, on the square. I shall never forget the years 1926 and the Miami storm. So many Henry Countians were in Miami at the time, among them my father, a sister, and three brothers. All communications were down, and it was several days before communications could be established and word could come through. Not once, did Ms. Berta leave her post until all Henry Countians had been accounted for, one way or the other.

I was a child of 10 years living on Carmichael Street in McDonough with my mother and the rest of my brothers and sister. Late in the afternoon of the third day, Ms. Berta called to say we had a telegram waiting. As I could run like a deer, my mother dispatched me to get it. As I ran into Ms. Berta's office, she looked up, smiled and said, "It's good news." The telegram read, "Thank God we are all safe. A letter will follow. Signed, Grace."

I am sure there are others who remember Ms. Berta as I do. She was my hero.

—Edna Evans Hammock

I tried to piece together the time frame of the telegraph's presence in our town. Aunt Berta was the only operator from the early 20's and all through the 30's to perhaps '39. Along about that time when telephones became more prevalent, they closed all the small telegraph offices. Aunt Berta was in the office until it closed, and she then began a new daily routine of helping to run Payne's Dairy.

Some years earlier when her brother went to Ohio, she and her husband moved into the large farmhouse with my grandmother. It took many hands to work the dairy. Various of Uncle Bob's nieces and nephews from time to time served in this capacity. Close to town, it enabled those who lived far out the opportunity to go to high school. Aunt Berta had taught telegraphy to a sister-in-law, and Mary, one of Uncle Bob's nieces. Both of them used it in their life's work.

She would rather cheat herself than to shortchange another. After she was widowed and ran a cattle farm herself, all who ever worked for her knew first-hand her fairness.

The example she set, not only for me but for her in-law relatives and others who had worked for her, was to share what you had, prepare yourself through education, and to do your best at whatever you were called to do. If anybody ever earned the respected title of Miss, she did.

⁂

"This is the way I remembered Aunt Berta those last days of her life, Father, when You gave me visions of her as young, vibrant with snapping brown eyes that spoke volumes. I am humbled and honored that I was permitted to be her niece and to walk a long way of my life with her close by."

Chapter 30
A Legacy to Keep

From the kitchen of the old homestead I progressed to Aunt Berta's bedroom to continue the task before me. I had approached it room by room sorting out a lifetime of her personal effects. They contained the treasures of two generations before her of my daddy's family.

The prospect of preserving the history of a goodly heritage was overwhelming. With no siblings, or even a cousin to share family memories, it was proving a painful experience for me.

When you are the last to carry the name of a long blood line, a greater sense of obligation in tying up all the loose ends presses upon you. Certain things must be finished once for all. It's your family with no one else to do it. So you must.

A sense of desolation filled the house. I fancied its walls sighed with the loneliness houses must feel when all the laughing voices have hushed, when all the footsteps are forever silenced. A chill hung in the air, and encased my heart in a frosty atmosphere of insecurity, indecision, and separation.

Somehow, I had always known it was part of my reason for being here. At the same time I couldn't shake a feeling of wanting to run, to shift the responsibility to someone else. "Why, Lord, must I always face the mountains alone?"

Aunt Berta had been my second mama. Still, I felt like an intruder going through her things. Aside from that, I grieved for the end of the once productive farm that for one hundred and sixty- seven years had taken care of my family.

Nostalgia lay thick and heavy everywhere I looked. Plowing gear still hung in the mule stable. On one of the harnesses, initials of a long ago field hand was carved into the leather.

In retrospect I could see the men and their mules move across the cotton fields acre after acre. From the distant echoes of memory, I could hear the clatter of milk cans, the clink of the bottles in yesterday's dairy, the activity of a busy working enterprise. Now forever stilled.

I remembered what Uncle Bob told me, "When houses and land have finished their purpose for a particular family it is time to let go. We are but stewards for a time." Mechanically, I was working toward that premise, but my heart wasn't cooperating.

It was then I saw Aunt Berta's worn flannel shirt lying across a chair. I picked it up to fold it away, but decided instead in the chill of the room to put it on. And in that simple act a strange thing happened. With the warmth of its covering, something inside me began to thaw, too. Odd that I would think it but Elisha came to my mind, how he had picked up the mantle of Elijah.

Walking to the window, squaring my shoulders and lifting my head, a new spirit took hold of me. Looking across the pasture it seemed God was giving me a sort of vision. I could see family members as they had walked here before me. Some of them had died before my earthly sojourn began. Even so, from having heard about them all my life, I could visualize them. It seemed each one was giving me a reason for being here. Although the family name would die with me the same blood flowed through me on into my children.

Suddenly, I remembered an object I had uncovered earlier, a giant ledger book. I leaned over the desk to pull it out, blowing dust from its ancient cover. Turning to a page where in beautiful Elizabethan script my grandmother had written long before my birth, I read, "The house burned January 21, 1921. We will build again." Farther on in my father's hand, "We began rebuilding today. This is a list of supplies." Then another I could readily relate to, penned under Cattle by Aunt Berta when I was a little girl, "I sold Bonnie and Shanks today. It broke my heart."

Incorporated within lined pages of the past were the joys, the sorrows, the everyday living, the decisions they'd had to make — the history and continuity of a family. In some peculiar way, I was not alone anymore.

True, the responsibility had been thrust upon me. The final countdown had to be my own. I accepted that; I'd always known it would come. There was a difference now. In the silent homestead God gave me a mantle of protection, the comfort of His presence. I had a legacy to keep, and I would wear the mantle with courage as those before me had worn it.

One day when I lay it down there would be another to pick it up. It is the natural order of life. Our past, whether a firm foundation to climb upon or ashes to arise out of, may be the catalyst that promotes tomorrow's potential. But our response is for today, as stewards of the present. That much, with God's help, I could handle. He had once again opened my eyes on my Emmaus Road.

I sat down at the desk. With the ledger before me, I turned to a clean page. With my pen I wrote, "With God we begin a new tomorrow...and we will not walk alone."

"From beloved people in my life I have many wonderful legacies, Lord. In their travels they have reached their destinations while I have yet a way to go. Thank You for the gifts of love they left me in road signs along the way. And thank You that You still accompany me."

Chapter 31
First Steps

I couldn't believe what the minister said. In the first place I couldn't believe Geneva was dead! But here I was at her funeral. The preacher told how Geneva had in more recent years worried about her salvation and wanted some reassurance about it. That's what I couldn't believe, for it was Jeanette and Geneva who first directed me to Sunday school and church.

Jeanette and Geneva were the twins who lived at the end of the wood's path during our high school years. We shared a lot of memories about the dairy and the things we often did between milking times.

In Ohio home was far out in the country. I had no way to go to church and only went on rare occasions. When I first came to Georgia to live with my grandmother I still didn't go to church. My grandmother, in her late eighties, didn't go anywhere much anymore and Aunt Berta was delivering milk during church hours. Cows have to be milked whether it's Sunday or Monday.

Along about then Jeanette and Geneva announced to me that I should be in Sunday School, and I could go to the Baptist Church where they attended. My family was Methodist.

However, since I knew the twins and would rather not go alone I started going to Sunday school with them.

Sometime after, during a revival Jeanette and Geneva walked down the aisle to accept Jesus as their Savior. I was close behind. If it sounds like I followed in their footsteps, it was not that way at all.

I had been an eager learner about this wonderful Jesus. And inasmuch as my thirteen year old understanding could take in, I knew I wanted to follow Him forever. When I asked Him to come into my heart it seemed as if a light was turned on inside of me. As indeed it was, and it has never gone out.

After our marriages the twin's paths and mine branched off in different directions. Geneva was far away raising her family in Wyoming. Jeanette and I raised ours in Georgia but we rarely saw each other. Even after Geneva moved back to her native state, we were not close like we had been as teenagers.

Still, there was always a tie that bound us. Besides having worked in the dairy together, we set out upon the path to follow Jesus at the same time.

Most important to me is how in the beginning God used them as the instruments who taught me the simple truth that I should be in Sunday school. I may have wandered around a bit on the road they pointed me to, and sometimes I side tracked down alleys I was not supposed to enter. But with gentle urging the same Jesus I embraced at thirteen would lead me once again toward the right direction.

Maybe Geneva felt she, too, had traveled down some of those questionable paths and wanted to be sure she set the record straight. I was glad she talked to her pastor. The last time I saw her, there seemed to be a different gentle peace about her, that in Jeanette had always been more visible.

Geneva's journey has ended. While she has left her Emmaus

Road, Jeanette and I have a way yet to go. However many miles mine may be, I do not forget that it was the twins who helped me begin with those first small steps in following our Savior.

"While others had a part, Lord, in helping me to experience a deeper faith in You, I know You hold into account that it was Jeanette and Geneva who led me to find You in the first place."

Chapter 32
Maw Maw's Narcissus

A few feet up the road from our house, built by Edwin's great-grandfather one hundred twenty six years ago, is the clearing where Edwin's grandfather and grandmother once lived. The house and outbuildings have long disappeared, but the tall oaks still stand.

And the narcissus still bloom every spring like they had been put out the year before, instead of over one hundred years ago. In 1911 the grandparents moved to their own farm west of this homeplace, leaving the narcissus behind in the yard of their first home.

It gives me a feeling of continuity as I visualize the young girl kneeling to place the small bulbs into the earth. She came there as a bride and all three of her sons were born there. It was home until they moved when her youngest was seven years old. By the time I became her granddaughter- in-law her husband was already gone, and her grandsons called her Maw Maw.

Every spring when the narcissus poke their heads through the soil, I watch for the blooms that soon will appear. It is a special time then for me of remembering Maw Maw.

She would tell us facts about the family, an oral genealogy of sorts. I'd nod and not pay attention and years later wished so much I had written down what she could recall. I like to think she would be pleased that eventually I became interested and actually got together enough of the family tree to put something of it in our county history book on first families.

She taught me things I hadn't known about sewing, and if I came upon a particularly difficult pattern she could help me figure it out. A lot of what I know about cooking I learned from her.

One of those I never thought I'd use was the way she prepared fresh creamed corn. She would run the blade of a sharp knife down the center of each row of kernels, going all around the whole ear. Then with the knife blade she would scrape the ear from top to bottom. It made extra creamy corn. We didn't care for it prepared that way, but the last summer of Edwin's life when he had such difficulty eating, I made his corn dishes like those his grandmother made. I almost felt as if she were still helping me and was so thankful I remembered how to do it.

The women of her day discussed other women who could "turn off a lot of work." If you could turn off work it meant you could get a lot done in a day. You were efficient and organized and there wasn't a lazy bone in your body.

Maw Maw was one of those. You also knew where you stood with Maw Maw. If somebody gave her a gift for which she had no use, she was apt to say, "I've got about as much use for this as a hog has a side saddle." No need for pretense.

If you took her along to visit someone, you knew she was going to need a drink of water so she could go into the homeowner's kitchen in order to check out her housekeeping. In her book cleanliness was indeed next to godliness.

She would have made a great police interrogator. In idle conversation she could find out all sorts of things about a person, with them totally unaware that they had given away all the family secrets.

If she was visiting one of us in her family and we left mail lying about, she thought it was her right to pick it up and read it. Her children, who considered her a 'character,' may have been horrified but to her it was all in the family and family members shouldn't have secrets from each other. Besides, it should encourage you to tidy up your paperwork.

Church attendance was important to her. The little country church she attended most of her life didn't have a full time preacher, but on the Sunday he preached you went to worship. Of course, you went to the church every Sunday for a Bible class taught by church members. She was active in the ladies missionary society of her church and took part in the programs. She may not have known how to pronounce some of those far away places, but she said you could call them what you wanted to. Who would know the difference? God knew who you were praying for anyway.

My mother lived hundreds of miles from us and was unable to come when I had my first baby. But Maw Maw lived just up the road. When Maw Maw's great-grandson was born she took care of him and me. In her day mothers who had just given birth stayed in bed for eight days. I convinced her it wasn't necessary, but I was truly grateful she came that first week and cooked us tasty meals, did the laundry, kept the house, and looked after both of us in general. I've never had such wonderful attention. When our second baby came along two and a half years later, Maw Maw was not able to come. I longingly thought of that earlier birth.

Maw Maw's narcissus reminds me more than anything that we all leave something of ourselves on this earth. She left the imprint of her strength and resilience. With her it was better to laugh than to cry. None of us are too good to pick up a hoe or shovel or whatever it takes to turn off the work. Take care of your own loved ones and send them off with a full tummy. Speak the truth and it may set you free.

It is true Maw Maw was a character but one I loved, and who was a great companion and helper on the Emmaus Road. She was always ready to lend a hand to anybody who needed an extra one.

"Dear God, thank You for Maw Maw's narcissus, although it doesn't take them to remind me of what a treasure she was to me. Thank You she was there when I needed someone older, wiser, with great humor but no nonsense. The narcissus are like Your love. They keep on forever."

Chapter 33
Light Within

The sanctuary of the little country church was shrouded in darkness. The congregation sat quietly awaiting the program to unfold before their eyes.

Seated at the piano, the church music director began to play softly. Wayne and Kerry came from the back of the building, each of them carrying a long white taper. Smoothly, their white robes flowing, the teen-agers moved in unison to the candles placed throughout the room, touching them briefly with flame from their own. Every lighting created a glow around it to meet the next circle until they all suffused together, merging into a soft, warm brilliance.

The candle lighting reminded me of the moment I accepted Jesus as my Savior when a light came on which has never gone out. I noticed something else that night. What happens when a lighted candle touches an unlighted one? It, too, is ignited but notice how some flicker and sputter giving a lesser light, while others burn tall and stately lending far more radiance.

Some Christians I have encountered along the way are radiant floodlights in spreading God's glory. Does that make those who have smaller flames any less in their plan and purpose? When you consider, for example, the total darkness of the inner recesses of a cave and someone strikes a match, the tiny flame seems to cast a beacon of hope.

For to the person who is in the total darkness of unbelief, even a tiny flicker may be all they need to find the true Light that Jesus offers. In John's Gospel chapter 1, verse 5 it says,"And the light shineth in darkness; but the darkness comprehended it not." I understand it to mean that there is absolutely no way darkness can put out the light which Jesus brought, for He is the Light.

For the person who has lost the way, or is weighed down with burdens of fear and worry, the smallest gleam can beacon them to a better path. It made me ask myself what I am doing to hold back the darkness.

In the acknowledgments of this book, I have listed ministers of the Gospel, who at certain intervals cast special light upon my Emmaus road. Without these shepherds of the fold in any of our lives, the path could be far more treacherous.

From my very first infant steps as a new believer, down through life's growing time, they gave immeasurable instruction and guidance. Each in their own unique way were the lighted candles in my life. Because of them and those like them, their ministry has shown us how to keep our candles lit and the wicks trimmed.

All of these taught me the importance of allowing the Light within to penetrate the darkness so others might be drawn to it. Jesus truly is that Light. It should become our burden and then our joy to see that none of those with whom we come in contact walk in darkness. Together our smaller lights make a continuously spreading circle. And that is our purpose, and the task He left us.

❧❀✦

"How thankful I am, Lord Jesus, for Your servants who strengthened and taught me as we walked down the years. Their glow shines radiantly. Many candles have been lighted from their flames. All because of You, Lord."

Chapter 34
Gehenna

After Great-Uncle Charlie died, Ruby and I cleared out his house. Even though family members received certain items a lot had to be discarded, which is always the case when someone has lived in the same place for decades.

Those things not useful we carted off to the city dump. At that time private citizens could drive into the area specified for refuse, empty their vehicle and drive out. With no attendant on duty, it appeared you could go wherever you could maneuver your way.

I'm not sure how Ruby, my husband's Uncle Troy's wife, and I got elected to perform this less than delightful task. Maybe it was due to the fact that together Ruby and I could get a lot of work done. We loaded Edwin's pickup truck and drove off to the dump.

Neither of us had been there before, and we were startled to find no attendant on hand to direct us. Back then garbage was burned not buried, so you just found a place that was not on fire. An eerie, depressing air hung about the place. We tossed the last of our load to the ground when we noticed a pile of bricks nearby.

We both had the same idea. Our young pastor lived in a mobile home next to our country church. His trailer could do with some underpinning, not only to keep out the cold but to improve its appearance. The bricks had been thrown away. Since we were the only bodies thereabout, no one was around whom we might ask. Our mutual decision was that God would be pleased if we took the bricks to our pastor. Anyway, nobody but us and God would know.

We were quite smudged and dusty by the time we got all the bricks loaded. They were heavy and it was hot, but we kept working until we loaded all of them. It was only then we noticed our position had become a mite perilous. The fires burning here and there had united. We were practically within the burning circle. The flames were low but you surely would not want to drive through them.

We took stock of our options and then with a maze-like run we drove out the gate to cooler and safer ground.

That was when Ruby said, "I believe that's a good example of the dump outside Jerusalem where they took their trash. Didn't Jesus liken it to hell?"

Later we would laugh about it. There we were in the fires of Gehenna, confiscating bricks not designated for us. You could say we were pilfering for God. We like to think they were labeled by our Lord for one of His servants. We were merely the instruments of their moving.

❧⟨✜⟩❧

"Ruby and Troy were special in our lives, Lord, as were Edwin's other Uncle Hope and his wife Lila, who helped us much in our younger years. Ruby and I worked together a lot as we made our way down Emmaus Road, and with Ruby there was always laughter. Thank You for pleasant companions along the way."

Chapter 35
The Rock

My daddy and I never got the chance to really get acquainted before he died. My five year old memory wasn't strong enough to recapture the experience of that relationship. Watching other kids with their dads, I felt left out. Even when they included me, I'd push away, shy and embarrassed.

I could picture a tall, lanky frame, I could see his floppy old straw hat, his smile. But I could not see my father's eyes, nor know his thoughts. A vague familiarity with him has always eluded me. To touch him, to see him, to hear his voice has long been a powerful force of longing in me.

Any scrap of knowledge about him I could glean I held close to my heart. People didn't talk about him much. They thought it would make us sad, and I lacked the courage to ask questions back then.

When I went to live with my grandmother, Aunt Berta, and Uncle Bob on Daddy's family farm in Georgia I thought here in the house where he had lived surely I would find some evidence of his having been here. I asked questions, but no matter how many I asked no one was able to satisfy my hunger to make him real.

Once I found his signature scrawled in a book. Another time I discovered a hand written entry in the farm's journal. I gazed at the markings in awe, longing for a sense of his presence.

Soon after, I found the rock. In a flower bed lay an oblong rock with the initials REW carved deeply into the stone. My daddy's initials! Tangible proof that he had been here! His hands, his effort, his strength had made an impression in the stone. I tried to envision him as he chiseled it out. How long had it taken? What did he use? Did he do it a little at a time after his chores were done, or had he finished it in one afternoon?

I ran my fingers along the roughly hewn edges, and then carefully, reverently replaced it among the flowers, where I felt he had placed it himself. I promised myself there it would stay. During the years of my growing up it gave me comfort and a feeling of his presence.

When I married and left my grandmother's house, I left the rock too. I felt it would be an intrusion to move it. I could revisit any time.

Eventually Daddy's sister, my beloved Aunt Berta, was the only one left at the home place. I would occasionally check on the rock, and had not changed my mind that it should remain in its special place. Why, this was the homeplace! It would always be there.

Years rolled by, a decade, two, my children were born, grown, and gone from home. Several decades. I had begun my fifth when at the very end of her eighth, Aunt Berta died.

With her leaving I inherited the responsibility and painful task of closing out a family homeplace which I could not afford to keep. I was thankful for my mother who lived in one of the houses on the farm.

One evening we sat on the back steps of the main house, and Mama helped me make the decision. She had made many moves in her life and was willing to make another. I told her I felt like I was selling my birthright. She said, "You do what you have to do. Your daddy would understand."

Thus began a process of clearing out barns and houses, sorting through treasures, some from the day of my great-grandparents. The most difficult of all was selling Aunt Berta's brood cows. I felt she probably would never forgive me for that.

Generations of living was removed from the premises of my family's farm. All loose ends were neatly tied together.

I had not forgotten the rock with the initials REW engraved upon it. The last thing I meant to do was to remove it from its place among the lilies. However, when I went to retrieve it, I discovered it was gone. I searched all over. How dare anyone remove it! But someone had.

For two weeks I continued my search, chiding myself for not taking it home with me years earlier. Silently I grieved; nobody could understand how much the stone with my daddy's initials meant to me. I pleaded with God, "Please help me find the stone." But I got no answer and had no success in my frantic search.

On the day before I signed the final papers, I made one last futile exploration. Close to the pear tree heavy with green fruit, I found an engraved stone. Or more exactly a chunk of stone and concrete with initials scratched in it. The initials were CWN. My own! More than forty years earlier in the foundation of a new storage building I had marked my initials. That little structure was long gone and here was this remaining chunk. I picked it up in awe.

I never found Daddy's rock. Was God telling me that each time has its own season? We are the "ongoingness" of whoever came before us. Perhaps God was saying that my daddy, REW, had finished his season, his time, and purpose. Now it was up to me, CWN, to go on from there. My time and purpose was not yet finished.

❦

"Dear Lord, without Your help I never would have made it through those difficult days. Only You could give me the strength where I learned more completely that I am never without You. Although it was only a short distance, I am grateful my daddy walked with me however briefly on this journey."

Chapter 36
My Best Friends

I'm pretty sure I wasn't raised by wolves or nurtured by gorillas, but like my ex-daughter-in-law, Donna, I do have a great affinity for God's animal kingdom. Donna's main concern is cats, feral and homeless ones. She cares so much that she and a friend founded and run an international organization called Alley Cat Allies.

I think I'm far more comfortable with four-legged creatures because they accept me as I am and ask little of me except a handout and a kind word now and then. Of course, I refer mostly to cats, dogs, and farm animals, though the wild ones trust me more than most.

One day at the creek I had a nice chat with a beaver I had surprised. He sat there and listened as I gave him news of the country. If the dogs are not with me the deer just sort of stand around and look at me when I talk to them.

People who don't care for animal kind, think them low in intelligence, understanding, and empathy. I have seen this proven far from true. Sometimes they seem to me more civilized than folks.

Our horse Powder, who wouldn't tolerate any other creature in his pasture, would nudge Caesar, our German shepherd, through the fence after he became arthritic. When Caesar was young, Powder would give him nasty nips on his tail.

If one of the kittens climbed into Powder's feed trough, he would gently pick it up in his mouth and carefully deposit it on the ground.

Our neighbors at this particular time had a big Weimaraner, who came into our yard one day and caught Sister Sue, one of my cats. Terrified, she limply hung from the predator's mouth. All my screeching and chasing just made him run faster.

Bootsy, my shy mixed breed, dashed around the house when he heard the commotion. Taking it in he realized, I'm sure, he couldn't fight that big dog. So he used the best method his age and size permitted. He charged across the yard and rammed his head into the usurper's side, using his little body like a battering ram.

The startled thief dropped his victim to gasp for breath and took off for home on the run. Bootsy had saved Sister Sue! That was intelligence, empathy, and bravery all wound together. After all, Sister Sue was family. Don't mess with the Nail cats and dogs!

Another time as soon as I stepped outside I could tell our two German shepherds and the three smaller fellows of mixed origin had discovered something unusual. They were rushing around trying to communicate to me in a big way that they had a little problem behind the barn they didn't know how to handle. No barking nor fuss. That was my cue to go see what was up.

I found her lying in a pathetic heap against a bale of hay. Appearance told me she was an old dog, type unknown. Her coat, the color and texture of a collie, was matted with dirt and blood. She had tangled with something—wild creature or another dog. Not ours though. They were concerned, almost like eager children urging me to see about this they had found.

She didn't flinch when I stooped tentatively to examine her, and seeing no sign of aggression I carefully checked her body. She wasn't injured seriously it seemed, just superficially, but she was worn out from whatever she had battled.

I carried her to the little shed in the orchard with all five of my menagerie trailing along. We were on a mission. They milled around while I fixed her a comfortable bed in the hay. She lay down with a thankful sigh. We left her there to rest for awhile. Later I went back with medicated cream and treated the places where the skin was broken.

That day and the next several, when I went out to take food and water I had five anxious helpers, all interested and intent on taking care of our elderly visitor. They never tried to steal her food, although they would steal from each other. I was amazed at their concern but it was pleasant to watch.

The dog wore no collar, and although I called around I was unsuccessful in finding where she belonged. Day by day I could see an improvement. It appeared she just needed to rest and regain her strength. She began to get up and walk around some as if testing herself.

In a day or so I was standing at the kitchen window when I saw her coming slowly, with evident purpose, to the back yard. I went outside and she came up to me. She stopped, directed a long intense gaze into my eyes and then turned to go.

Something told me not to stop her going. My faithful five had joined me and we all silently stood and watched her progress across the field. It was with such determination, I knew I had to let her go for I sensed she was going home.

I was impressed she came out of her way from the orchard shelter to find me before she left. Her eyes told me, "I appreciate what you have done, but I must be getting home now."

She disappeared into the woods and I felt it was the last we'd see her. But one day on my way to town, I saw her again. She was sitting on the porch of a small white house like it was where she was supposed to be.

Normally, our five protectors chased away every dog that came onto the farm. It was part of their job. Somehow they felt this one was different. Perhaps her age? They were all younger. I can't explain it at all; it's just more proof to me that animals do have feelings similar to our own. Also they use some of the same practices. The day she left, our visitor came to thank me. You can't tell me otherwise.

❦

"Thank you, Father, for the special ones You have sent our way. Some of them have come so mysteriously it could only be from You. They are all a part of my forever family. When they must leave me one by one certain others take their place, as we walk along Emmaus together."

Chapter 37
In the Cloud

The cloud bank wrapped us in a smothery cocoon. I could see nothing beyond the vapor all around us. Uneasy, I looked over at my husband. He showed no evidence of alarm. Instead, he watched the instrument panel more closely, and gave me a reassuring smile. By radio he requested permission to change altitude.

I could feel the aircraft begin to climb as he nosed the Cherokee upward. Then I knew he meant to get above the cloud that enveloped us. It seemed to me we would fly through the strange cottony world forever. Suddenly, we broke through the mist and came out on top where the world was clear and beautiful again.

My husband was an excellent pilot. We jokingly referred to him as one of the "cotton patch boys," those accomplished fellows who can fly into and out of almost any tiny airstrip or pasture. I had not feared his proficiency. What I had not trusted was what I could not see. In contrast, he relied on the instrument panel and depended upon his skill and ability to follow its guidelines. I sometimes find myself in a cloud engulfed experience. I can only see what immediately surrounds me. I am fearful and do not trust myself to take the proper direction. Nor do I seem able to receive any hints from God. It's as if my inner hearing is clouded over as well.

Aunt Berta used to refer to certain individuals whose intelligence she questioned as someone "with not the sense God gave a goose." It was apparent she thought God had not given much of that quality to geese. On such murky days in my life, I can easily relate to that quality in myself.

In contrast I think of that particular day in the plane and Edwin's confidence. He relied on the instruments before him, but he also believed himself competent to deal with what he knew. Perhaps he believed he had more than goose sense.

Constantly I must remind myself that I need to be more secure in the ability God has given me. Besides, we all have before us God's Holy Word, a perfect instrument panel with all the right configurations. Because I am His child I can place my trust in it and in the guidance He is sure to give when I truly seek. I don't have to stay in the fog.

That's my prompt to request a change of altitude. While it may be by means we could never imagine, He always answers a sincere request. Then in much the same way as Edwin nosed the plane upward, God enables me to pull up and out of the cloud of confusion.

※⟨⟩❋

"Thank You, Lord Jesus, for showing me something special that day with Edwin in the Cherokee. It helps me to think of Your Holy Word as my instrument panel, the most important possession I carry on this road of life."

Chapter 38
You Can Dust

I was fifty two years old. I'd just had major surgery. Prior to releasing me from the hospital next day, the doctor had finished giving me the do-nots. Now she was on the can-dos. "You can attend your personal needs, you can cook, you can dust...."

I tried to look interested, like I was listening. But I cringed inside.

When I was little I'd watch Mama attack the house dirt with powerful sweeps of her broom. Or I'd hang over the dish pan while she performed magic swishes on the dishes in their soapy suds. I'd ask, hopeful I might be given a really important job like that, "Mama, what can I do?" And she would smile and say, "Well, let's see, Honey...oh, you can dust."

In fifth grade I watched a talented classmate make our story book characters come alive with her colored pencils on big paper sheets the teacher tacked up around the wall. I wanted to do something really big like that, too! I would ask, "What can I do, Miss Jackson?" And she would say, "Well, let's see...you can dust."

Early in our married life my husband would charge off to the fields on his magnificent machines. I wanted to do that, too. When I mentioned it he would say, "Well, you can hoe." In my estimation hoeing was a few pegs lower than dusting.

That's where I always seemed to be. One peg lower than I wanted to be. It's true the dusting and the hoeing in this life must be done. Why must it always be me who had to do them? They were such unimportant jobs, I felt cheated.

In time I found the dish pan, the broom, even the tractor didn't hold the glamour I long ago envisioned. I had raised a family, and along with miles of dusting I had tucked away a few accomplishments. I didn't feel cheated anymore, but I never made friends with dusting.

Now here this young lady surgeon was telling me I could dust. I had come full circle.

I was still feeling a little nettled when later I walked down the hall. Ahead of me a floor polisher whistled a happy sounding tune as he navigated the machine back and forth across the tile. When he stopped to move the electric cord down farther, I commented on his shiny floor.

"Yes, ma'am," he smiled. "Makes me feel good to look back down the hall and see how it shines! Can't nobody do my job like I can. God expects me to keep this floor clean so that's what I do."

He said it with such pride, I could tell he felt it was an important job. Had it been me I would have fumed inside that it was in the same boat as dusting.

Back in my room I lay in the hospital bed and thought about what he had said. He was absolutely right. Can't nobody do our job like we can. Guilt gave me a pretty good stab along about then when I remembered something that happened a few days earlier.

At that time the practice was to check into the hospital the night before surgery. I was standing at the hospital window and could see high above us geese on their journey to nesting grounds. They were on the way to their particular job. At that moment I wanted to be anywhere but in that hospital. Even the dusting would have looked good. Now here I was blessed to have the surgery behind me, and doing well. It was time to thank God, go home, and dust!

"Thank You, Father, for what the floor polisher told me that day. He only shared a minute or two of my Emmaus journey but he gave me something exceptional. I know now it's not what we do, but how we carry it out."

Chapter 39
What's in the Barn?

I am told it is good practice for a writer to keep a daily journal. That I do. However I think it's due more to survival therapy than anything else. It helps me keep up with things I can't remember. It unloads the steam and frustrations which plague us all.

This morning I was searching in one of them for something from another year, and came upon the frustrating time when my mother was slipping into some form of dementia. It was such a heartbreaking time. No matter how much I loved her and strove to make her life simpler, less confusing, there were times when I felt neither one of us was going to make it. My daughter maintained her grandmother could try the patience of Job. And I was no Job.

In town the other day I was happy to see my old friends Cleveland and Bessie, and was reminded anew of what a blessing they had been to me—and most particularly to Mama—during that stretch of my mother's life. For hours, they would listen patiently as she told the same stories over and over, yet they remained her friends.

The worst thing I had to deal with was myself and the shock and grief I experienced in seeing my once capable, strong mother become so different. I can close my eyes and see her handling with great expertise a rowdy horse. Or see her neat house with a place for everything and everything in its place. If you needed something she could put her hand right on it. I see her gentle hands soothing a sick old person, her humor in even the darkest moments, her generosity in sharing part of what she had, even if it wasn't much.

Leafing through my journal I came across an entry made soon after her dog, Prince, had died. I dug his grave myself in 90 degree weather. She helped me bury him. After that she would periodically hunt him, call me to tell me she couldn't find him. Each time my reminding her was enough to clear the confusion, and it would be fine for awhile. She also had a strange obsession that she had clothes stored in the barn. The entry for that day went something like this:

'September 21, 1990: Got most of my own chores out of the way before going to do Mama's. I must admit I have to get myself psyched up before going, for I never know what will come next. Today I worked on her clothesline. Even though she has a drier, she likes the smell of clothes on the line. She helped and we did okay together, the best we could do with the twisted wire. At least the four wires run untwisted to their proper hooks. Prince has been dead and buried for some time now. At least three or four times a week she hunts him. Today when she mentioned him I headed her off at the pass. Sometimes I can recall the moment for her. Sometimes it works. This time I got him buried again before the hunt began. It is most exasperating and sad. I know she misses him. So do I, but I get tired burying him over and over again.

Next she asked me if I'd help her find those clothes packed away in the barn. Usually I talk her out of it, but today with a little extra time I decided maybe if I went down there with her, it would be positive proof for her that no clothes were there. Or maybe I could figure what's bugging her about stored clothing. On the way her discourse went from a box to a barrel to garbage cans, to dirty laundry, to those ironed neatly and packed away.

We started on boxes. There were several mostly empty ones and a couple that held styrofoam popcorn. She poked and looked. She'd say, "Something's in that one." We took them down, we looked in each one. We found nothing. No barrels or garbage cans at all. She's so confused about the clothes. Back at the house she talked about Tiny, the dog she had when I was born. What happened to a dresser she and my daddy had? We traveled back to Newtown, to Anchor, to Columbus, all places where she lived.

She seemed to recall things correctly as we went on; she traveled with me quite well. When she'd hit a snag I'd help her remember. I felt we were on a roll and she was really comprehending. She seemed like Mama again and we were just reminiscing.

Back in the kitchen again, she leaned up against the cabinet and said, "Now I've got to go down to that barn and find those dirty clothes." Do I scream and cry, or just burst out laughing?'

❦

"Father, today please help all care givers, especially those who deal with muddled minds. It's such a hard path to travel for both of them. It's so painful to see loved ones change before your very eyes. Clear the fuzziness and hold them close. Forgive me when I wasn't always patient with my mama. But my love for her and Your love for us both led us safely down that troubled section of road."

Chapter 40
Forever Friends

As we sat around the table laughing and talking about our present days, I was reminded how far we have traveled together. Three of them I have known since I came to Georgia to live. Teen-agers then, all nearly the same age, over the years we have shared much and never lost touch.

Our friendships of long standing are interwoven into a tapestry not yet finished, except for Joann whose time here recently drew to a close. It makes me cherish all the more our last times together.

All of our families were among the first settlers in this county. I began to piece together our connections. Our husbands were boyhood friends. Frances married Jean's brother and Jean married Frances' brother. Catherine married Jean's cousin. My Aunt Berta and Frances and Joann's mother had been girlhood friends and remained so down the years. All of our husbands served in the armed forces either during or soon after World War II. Between us we bore eight children — three girls and five boys. Except for Catherine who has four, the others have two grandchildren each and I have two step grandchildren.

We were friends in a time when people set down their roots and stayed in one location most of their lives. Could it be that this type of tie we share is in danger of disappearing because our world is now so fast moving?

Roots don't have time to spread as deeply as they once might have. That's not to say those relationships which come and go more quickly in our lives are less meaningful and deep. Some special people may walk with us only a short distance, while others are there for most of our lifetime.

What has this to do with my Emmaus Road? An intangible bond cements me with these lives who have been my forever friends. In and out of my days they have walked along with me as they make their way along Emmaus as well.

Few secrets are kept from those who know you so well, and yet love you warts and all. We have cried together and we can still laugh together. We tell each other how grateful we are to still know who we are, and that we know the way to go home.

They have been my sisters when I needed a sister, my confidants when I needed to share, my sounding board when I needed to blow off steam, my shoulder to cry on when my burden was heavy.

God provides particular people for us as our years spread out behind us and before us! Some we are privileged to know only briefly. Others, for all our days. It makes the way so much easier and so less lonely. Cherish those who know you best.

≈≫⟨✦⟩≪≈

"May You bless these dear and long time friends, Father, and continue Your walk with those of us who remain. Treat them kindly and help each one to draw closer and closer to You, and thank You that I am privileged to know them."

Chapter 41
Edwin's Here

The last year of Mama's life when she was often confused, I worried she'd accidentally set fire to her house. For years she had heated the whole house with a wood heater and a blower. I hoped I had convinced her to let the gas furnace do the work instead. Still, I worried.

At night the sitters took care of her safety. In the daytime I did it myself. Her house was close by and I would run in and out several times a day, plus check with her by phone. She could still use the phone and take care of personal needs. Mostly she just forgot to cook, or take a bath. Time had always been irrelevant to her. With age it just got worse.

She was grateful for the things I did for her and always let me know it. However, when it came to replacing a loose door knob or unstopping a washer hose, she wanted Edwin to do it. I ran myself ragged attempting to do all the chores I could in order not to bother my husband, a busy man, with my mother's problems. But she never believed anything I repaired was truly fixed. Some things I couldn't take care of and would have to call on Edwin. The morning I set fire to her house was one of those times.

I had gone over rather early. She was eating breakfast while I finished up her house chores. Just prior to leaving I noticed a large empty cereal box sitting on the hearth. 'Oh no,' I thought, 'she'll have that thing in the heater and it will create too much of a blast.'

I stuck it in the heater myself and lighted it, thinking to get rid of it before she noticed. Then I thought of something else I needed to do. It took longer than I expected. When I came back to the sitting room I heard a tremendous roar. Horror stricken, I realized I had left the draft fully open and now the chimney was on fire!

I ran outside to see flames shooting out the top of the chimney. I ran back inside to call Edwin. Thank heaven he was home and came right over. Mama was sitting at the kitchen table calmly eating her breakfast even though I was running around like something demented. I suggested she go outside and she just looked at me and kept eating her breakfast.

Edwin got the ladder and the water hose and went up onto the roof. By now I couldn't see flames shooting out the top it's true, but I was alarmed when Edwin just sat down next to the chimney. Why wasn't he spraying water down it? When I screeched the question up to him he said it would be better not to hose it since the blaze was dying down considerably.

I couldn't believe my ears and ran back into the house to get my mother out. She had left the table and was sitting in a rocker in front of the heater, calming drinking a cup of coffee and looking at the morning mail.

"Mama!" I'm sure I screamed at her for she looked up at me like I'd lost my last mind. "Mama, you need to come outside with me. Didn't I tell you the chimney's on fire?"

She just took another sip from her cup, leaned back in her chair and said, "Well, Edwin's here isn't he?"

Edwin's here. Edwin will take care of it. Edwin will know how to fix it. If I had been taking care of it, she would have gotten as far away from the house as possible.

Since I loved them both it didn't really hurt my feelings that she had no more confidence in me concerning the larger problems. I am grateful she trusted her son-in-law to that extent. What she sensed about him was the same with each person who knew him well.

One day when several of us were in question as to how a certain situation could be handled one of the men said, "When Edwin gets here he'll know what to do. He'll figure it out."

An assurance emanated from him which dispelled uncertainty and fear from those in his presence. He did possess a great ability to figure things out. He repeatedly would tell me, "Study whatever it is. Look at it, try to reason how it works."

When we knew his time here was limited he spoke aloud one of his desires, "If I could just leave the knowledge in my head and the skill in my hands to someone else." It was said with humility, not conceit. He longed to transfer his gifts to someone else if it were possible.

Edwin is not here now. Those times I so desperately need him to be I try to practice some of the things he told me. Most of all I remember that I am not alone. The God who gave Edwin such great ability takes care of his loved ones.

I need to strive for serenity of spirit like Mama had when she sat in front of the heater, confident that the man of the family would handle the problem.

Edwin is not here. Even when he was he knew he didn't have the power or strength for everything. But God does have all we require or need. It is safe to put our trust in Him. He is here.

❦

"Both Mama and Edwin have left me, Lord. It wasn't their fault they had to go. You said it was time. You have helped me accept it, and now I walk toward Emmaus without them. Thank You they were able to travel as far as they did. Their strong influence propels me forward."

Chapter 42
Special Delivery

On the day Mama died a peculiar thing happened which I have shared with few people. It had been an ordinary sort of day. As usual Mama had prepared her own breakfast of cereal, coffee, and usually a sweet roll, her favorite.

I went over to her house to attend the house needs. We changed the bed linens together with talk of ordinary things. She told me again about a parakeet she saw in the bush outside her window. I explained as before that parakeets didn't live in the wild in our area. In ten minutes she was telling me the same story.

Her house was just down the road from mine which made it easy to run in and out all day. Still capable of using the phone, she called me several times a day. If I didn't hear from her my practice was to check on her.

Late that afternoon she called to say she had received an important letter and wanted me to come over to see about it. Quite active, she made the trip down the long drive to the mailbox and back up the hill to her house. The mail each day was a big event. I told her I was preparing her supper and would be there in a few minutes. I knew it probably wasn't an important letter.

Thirty minutes later I unlocked her back door, calling to her as I entered. I could see her from the L-shaped kitchen into her living room where she sat on the sofa like I often found her sound asleep. She held the letter in her hand. I called to her, "Mama, I'm here with your supper." I repeated it several times while I laid the dinnerware.

"Mama, you're really having a nap today aren't you?" I said as I stepped in front of her and placed my hand on her arm. She felt different somehow. I dropped to my knee and looked into her bent over face, and realized with a shock she was not breathing.

Long ago she had ordered no resuscitation. I couldn't think whether you had to call 911 anyway. I dialed Bill, the neighbor between us, who was there in seconds. After he made the call, I suggested he take his dogs, who had followed him, home before the EMTs arrived. It gave me a few minutes alone with my mother for the last time.

I took Red, her large Irish setter-Saint Bernard mix, to her bedroom. He had been standing guard over her body and I knew he would not allow strangers to touch her. When I returned from the bedroom, I knelt once again at her feet and laid my head on her knee, hoping to draw some comfort from her. I felt so alone and bereft. Even though I knew her choice would be to go quietly, I could hardly breathe with the crushing weight of grief upon my chest.

It was when I lifted my head that I saw something I had never, ever seen, or even heard about. All around her body was an aura, a rosy hue that surrounded her and hovered over her. It was an awe-filled moment and I felt she and I both were bathed in a Holy Presence.

Later and many times since I have questioned if I was

hallucinating. But it was too real. I know what I saw. For a long time I didn't tell anyone; it does sound illusory. Then one summer I shared it with my cousin, Clarene, and she said she had also seen such an aura over a deceased friend.

What did it mean? Why don't we see it every time? I don't have any answers at all. I only know it was an experience I shall not forget.

After Mama's funeral, when we took Red home with us, he adapted better than I anticipated. Her cat, Tibby, kept going back home. She would stay with us a day or two and then she'd disappear; I knew where to find her. She'd be curled up at the door or under a bush in the front yard waiting for Mama to let her in. Each time I'd get her fur all wet with my tears.

I was grateful my mother didn't live to become more infirm. At the same time I missed her dreadfully. Although her memory failed, her humor didn't. She would find something to laugh about even in trying situations. I felt I would never laugh or feel happy inside again. I talked to God about it, but it didn't make me feel much better.

Then one afternoon when I felt particularly low Edwin came into the kitchen and said, "You'll never guess what I have." He came up close behind me where I was standing at the sink. He was right. Never in a million years would I have guessed what he gently held.

Nesting comfortably in his big hand was the most beautiful green and yellow parakeet I'd ever seen. While coming across the yard he felt something alight on his shoulder. Thinking it was a leaf, he reached up to brush it off. Instead he closed his hand around this wonderful creature, who seemed extremely happy to have found us.

Recalling Mama's insistence that she had seen a parakeet outside her window Edwin said, "Well, your mom has had the last word again."

It was a fantastic moment that multiplied into millions more. Bebop became a special part of our family and with his entertaining antics once more brought laughter into my life.

We have no idea how far he traveled. We know he had not come from anyone close by. In my heart I am firmly convinced that he was sent from a loving Heavenly Father who knew I needed some cheer in my soul. I think he was sent by very Special Delivery.

❧

"I marvel at Your perfect and beautiful creations, Father. What joy Bebop brought to all of us for the seven and a half years he was with us on our journey! Thank You for his bright, and happy, and most intelligent presence. And thank you that I learned to laugh again."

Chapter 43
Paths

Paths of all sizes run in different directions all over our farm. The horse has his own private lanes to chosen drinking spots at the creek, where water collects in little pools. The beavers waddle along muddy trails from young saplings to various lodge entrances in their beaver pond. It is easy to follow the deer paths, distinguished by the trees where they stop to scratch their heads, and rub old antlers away. The foxes and other smaller animals scoot under low branches and leave tufts of hair on the barbed wire fence. Rabbits have tiny runs through the brambles.

When flushing birds in the wild grass the dogs run ahead helter skelter across the field. But when we start home everybody gets back to the narrow pathway we have been following. If you are in front, they trot close to your heels. To go around would get you off the prepared way, which to them must be unthinkable.

Strange how significant a path is to all things. Instinctively we will follow existing ones rather than make our own. There is something magic about seeing a worn trail that triggers a response to walk that way. Perhaps, it speaks of safety and promise because it is a known course.

Sometimes though the known way can be concealed. I recall a rainy season when water covered the little bridge on our dirt road to the highway. It happened whenever we had heavy rains, and I could never bring myself to cross it when the stream was flooded, although people like my husband had no problem with it.

On this particular morning it was necessary that I go to town. Since Edwin and I were going in different directions that day, he told me I could follow him to reach the pavement of the highway. "There will be nothing to it," he said.

I finally agreed and stopped on the way to pick up Roy, my neighbor, who wanted to go to town with me. I made the approach to the creek, slowly down the mud slick hill. I watched Edwin in the truck ahead skillfully maneuver his way across. Now it was my turn. The usually calmly flowing brook, swirling with muddy turbulence had become a wide, raging river. I panicked and stopped. No matter what, I couldn't bring myself to deliberately drive into it. My husband, realizing what had happened, got out of the pickup now safely on the other side to give me encouraging motions to move across. But I couldn't! Silently I wailed, "Lord, you know I can't do it."

I could tell my husband's patience was running out. His urging became a trifle more emphatic. Yet I sat like a frozen lump of clay, shaking my head, and whispering, "No, no." I couldn't tell where to drive! My old friend and neighbor beside me quietly took it all in. Then he spoke. "You know the bridge is still there. Someone has gone ahead to show you the way. Trust it. Use that tree there as a gauge and go on."

His reassurance gave me the courage I needed. I eased the car across the bridge which was still there, just as he promised. While I couldn't see the road ahead, it had not vanished.

Other times there might be hurdles in the road obstructing our way. Wayne was around three years old the day we were making our way across a plowed field to join his daddy on the far side. The plow had left big chunks of turned soil which we had to step over. It wasn't as hard for my long legs, but his short ones were giving him trouble as he huffed and puffed, stepping high. He said, "Boy, if these chunks was outta the way, I could sure walk better."

Both incidents helped me to understand if God has set me upon a certain course, even when the road may be blocked by obstacles, or screened from my sight, He will help me find the right approach to navigate my way and step high over the blockages.

Also, I am reminded to guard the way I walk. Should someone follow the path that I tread, it is my responsibility to mark a good trail, one that will not lead them astray.

⁂

"Whether I follow or lead someone else, it is comfort beyond measure to know You, Lord Jesus, lead the way for each of us. Thank You for all the paths to somewhere."

Chapter 44

In the Hall of the Barn

In our family the hall of our barn has strangely been the site for special experiences for three of us. I say, "strange" because it's such an unassuming place. We call it the barn. Actually, it is more like a long machinery shed, functional but without beauty.

Edwin had removed the loft of what had been two huge barns and joined them into a long building under one tin roof. Beginning from the north end, there are four enclosed rooms, five open bays and an airplane hanger at the south end. I describe this building for it is the setting for my story. But first we must go back a few weeks.

For a long time we worked so diligently at being positive, even hopeful, that we fought facing the truth. I think all of us secretly feared the worst in the last months of Edwin's illness. I know it clutched at my heart like a vise sapping the strength from any reserve I may have had. Then exactly one month and four days to his death, we made our last trip to Edwin's oncology surgeon, Dr. Stephen Auda.

At first while he was cleaning the wound behind Edwin's ear, the surgeon spoke of more surgery. Then Dr. Auda went out to see more patients and in a little bit I heard him tell the nurse to have me go to his office. It sounded ominous. Before he got there I had time to compose myself somewhat.

When he came in he told me they could try more surgery but there was no way they could get to all the cancer behind the carotid artery. Nor did he think Edwin would live through another operation in his debilitated condition. What he wanted to know was: should we tell Edwin or not? He said some people could handle knowing and some could not.

It only took a minute for me to know what we had to do. I told him I didn't think we had the right to keep it from my husband. He said, "Shall we tell him together?"

I have always been grateful God gave me the wisdom that day to allow truth to take over. It opened the floodgates for Edwin, the children, and me to uncover all our fears and heartbreak. Somehow just bringing them into the light helped us deal with them more productively.

Edwin was able to admit he was worn out with pain. He did not want any more surgery. He was given the chance to thank the doctor for giving him seven good years after the first primary cancer, and for the valiant fight he waged against this second one.

At home we talked a long time, sharing many thoughts and fears. I admitted to him I was scared and without him I didn't know how I could go on. He told me he would help me, that we had time to get a lot of things in order. That's how it came about that Brenda and I began to write down all we could remember to ask, and all he could remember to tell us about the farm and the equipment. She named it our Encyclopedia of Farming.

Edwin said he had already made his peace with God about leaving. He battled it out in the hallway of the barn next to one of his tractors and finally accepted that his earthly time was near its completion. He assured me I would be all right and would yet experience some good things.

At the time Wayne lived hundreds of miles away in Maryland, so most of it was up to Brenda and me. We had always helped with the farm work but it was done under Edwin's supervision. Whatever the particular task, we didn't have to worry about the care of the machinery, nor what made it tick. We had a lot to learn.

Many people have asked why we didn't just dispose of everything. Why worry about plowing and planting and machinery problems? We have asked ourselves that, too. We have our answers. Not only do we enjoy the fresh produce we freeze and can — enough for three households to last a year besides what we sell and give away — it goes much beyond that. Much farther back to 1821, when Wayne and Brenda's great-great-great grandfather sunk his first plow into this soil.

The little we do now is such a meager thing beside what this farm once produced. In our early years Edwin and I cultivated every inch of the open fields, rented two other farms, and planted all we could on them.

When I climb up on the tractor and start across a field I begin to talk to Great-Grandpa Nail and the greats before him. If they can hear me they may think what a pitiful attempt I make at it. But I believe they would be proud we still strive to be stewards of this land where God has blessed this family.

I talk to Edwin too. Of course, he can't answer me. I know it's the Holy Spirit who gives me the comfort and guidance required.

If I thought my husband could tell me, there are about a million questions I would ask. I miss his level head and his sensible advice. I've always talked to Edwin. Talking to him, even though it's only on my side, gives me a sense of connection to what we once had, and a peace of sorts. On occasion it helps me figure things out. I use his advice to study the situation, look it over, see how it works.

I haven't achieved success but I am still learning. I can change all the three point hitch and hydraulic equipment by myself. I admit it is a lot easier when Brenda and I can do it together. We've learned how to change the oil in the tractors and other machinery, how to grease all the grease fittings, things we never had to give a thought to. Brenda can manicure a field with the bushhog mower better than most. Edwin had time to prepare us for a great many tasks. But not all.

A small piece had broken off one side of the new planters. From the tractor company, where Jackie and Chase treat me with the same respect they do their men customers who know how to do these things, I got the new part. It was small and uncomplicated looking. All I had to do was remove a little screw or something, take out the broken section, and refasten the new one.

I chose the wrong time to do it. I was already tired and pressured. But it was just a little thing; I could change it in a matter of minutes. I got the screwdriver and set out to do it. The planters were in the main hall of the long barn, where Edwin had told me he relinquished himself to God's will.

While the children and I had absorbed a great deal involving the farm equipment, where the mechanics are involved I am still illiterate. I discovered when I got to the planters that the work required pliers rather than the screwdriver. What I had to take out was a cotter pin. Simple it was not. I tried and tried and the thing would not budge. I was overwhelmed with frustration. It wasn't fair! I worked hard to do these things myself and not bug somebody else. Why wouldn't it work?

Finally in futile frustration and a dose of self pity, I knelt in the hall of the barn and cried. I was too tired, too hot, too determined to handle more than I could cope with. In my journal on that day I wrote:

> As I knelt there in defeat, I asked God, "Why can't I do this little thing needing done? Why don't you help me?" I remember saying, "Please, God, if Edwin could help me, just for a little while."
>
> It sounds unreal, even to me, but when I wiped my nose and got up to try again, it truly felt like Edwin was there patiently saying, "That is not the right way. There is a bolt that goes through it—you don't remove the cotter pin. You undo the other side — see, that nut on the gear there?"
>
> I got the wrench that fit the nut, loosened it easily and when I did, I could push it through to the other side. It all came out, and sure enough it was a long bolt. When I put the new piece on I couldn't get the bolt through it. Again, the message, "Go to the drill press and make the hole bigger. Take the bolt so you'll know when it's right." I did. It worked beautifully. From there I got it all back together!

Now—to this receiving—it is hard to believe. I promise you it happened just as I wrote it later the same day. The directions came into my unmechanical mind. It is true Edwin always told me to study the situation and to figure it out. I did try, but without any success; it looked to me that the cotter pin needed to be removed.

I don't understand it; I can't fathom the mind of God. Perhaps if we listened more at desperate points of our lives…all I know is God gave this to me. I felt the familiarity of my husband, his calm "do it this way." I have no answers for any of it. But I believe God can do whatever He wants in order to bring us closer to Him. And this incident gave me that.

I said three of us had a special experience in the hall of our barn. On the day her daddy was dying, Brenda also went there filled with anger that we could do nothing to save her once powerful and strong father. As she prayed, God gave her a beautiful encounter which brought her to new understanding and acceptance.

God can speak to us in magnificent cathedrals. He can also speak to us in unpretentious places like rusty tinned buildings. Didn't his greatest gift to mankind lay in the sweet hay of a humble stable?

⚜

"I am awed and humbled by Your Presence, Lord Jesus, when I knelt defeated in the dust that day. Thank You for understanding our pain of loss, and for granting comfort in unique ways on our journey down the road."

Chapter 45
If a Bee Can

While I don't often have them, the doldrums had settled over me like a heavy cloak. It seemed a good time to sit down on the back steps and wallow in frustration and low self esteem.

I'd always worked hard and tackled most anything which came my way. Now with Edwin gone a lot more came my way. The children helped when they could but I tried not to burden them with what I considered my responsibility. Pulled to and fro by one obligation after another, my lifelong goals seemed to grow more remote. I honestly had little time left over for any forging ahead.

Besides, how much time did I have left? I felt incomplete, not finished yet, and frustrated because of it. Yet I couldn't stop the interference and routine chores that were forever getting in my way.

I knew part of my problem stemmed from my inability to accept and adjust to any type of interruption. Instead, I let the sidetracks warp my usefulness.

Suddenly, in the midst of this pity party, a powerful buzzing caught my attention. Closer inspection revealed a bumblebee had fallen into a bucket of water. Staying afloat by zooming his motor, he sped around like a miniature hydroplane. His determination prompted me to flip him out with a stick, where he plopped down on the ground exhausted. He was on his own now; his resuscitation was up to him.

In a little while he began to clean his waterlogged self. He wiped his face, scratched his tummy, and gave his wings a curious shake. A pause in the sun and he appeared ready for lift-off.

He tried, but couldn't quite get it together. When I realized his crawling around was an attempt to climb to something higher, I gave him another boost with the lifesaving stick. That did it. With a mighty thrust of his little engine he was airborne at last.

Bumblebees are fascinating specimens. Encumbered by early principles of aerodynamics, scientists maintained for decades that they could not possibly fly. With my elementary understanding of the fundamentals of aviation, that means their back half is too heavy for the size and reach of their wings. However, the bee doesn't know all the whys and wherefores of flying either. Therefore, he can fly. He isn't bogged down by any limitations he has set, or any which somebody else has made for him. God made him to fly, so he does.

When this particular bee got in a predicament, he refused to sink. Even though his speeding around wasn't getting him out, it was keeping him up. He wasn't going down without a struggle.

Neither did he reject the boosts I lent. He didn't spend a lot of time bowing with obligation, but I think a little communion passed between us. I could almost hear him say, "Whee, thanks a bunch!" Well, at least he didn't sting me when he got his second wind.

After a brief renewal he began to prepare himself to take up where he left off when interrupted by his watery plunge. You could tell he was concentrating his whole effort toward that point. Enough time had been wasted already.

He knew nothing about excuses for not doing his best, so he gave none. Getting back into action was enough compensation and motivation to keep him going. He wanted to do it so he did — he was supposed to do it. That was half the battle won.

Even a simple bee creature had handled his interruption like part of a larger plan, making it work for him and benefitting from its delay.

I had just received one of the best sermons I'd ever heard. As the bee bumbled away out of sight he took my gray mood with him, and left in its place some practical and useful insights.

Each one of us—critter or human—has the same twenty- four hour slices of time. It's how we meet and use it that makes the difference. When an interruption comes along, we need to remember it is only a pause in time. Sometimes it may even be by God's appointment.

Properly chastened I began preparing myself to take up where I had left off when I was plunged into the miseries. God had just given me a boost up.

❦

"Father, I realize some people will think a bee can't expound a proper sermon but I know You used one on this particular day when I needed a special lift. Thank You for meeting my need in a way I could grasp at the time. And thank You for unique creations who travel with us through this life."

Chapter 46
Neighbors

The dictionary states that a neighbor can mean our fellow man, but the general term is 'one who lives close by.' I am told there are good neighbors and bad neighbors. You may have encountered some of the latter, but more important is to ask ourselves which category we fit.

My first experience learning about neighbors was back in Ohio with Nannie and Granddaddy. Jojo had immigrated from Italy as a younger man, though he still spoke only halting English. Except to sell the produce he grew, he pretty much kept to himself. Behind his small dwelling he had a wonderful grape arbor.

Despite speaking different languages, he and Granddaddy had struck up a friendship. They were able to communicate well enough that each year Jojo invited his neighbor to help him prepare his grapes for the wine he made for himself.

I particularly remember one occasion of "readying the grapes for wine". Granddaddy went down to perform his annual assistance. It seems that after the grape stomping and whatever else you did to make wine, the final step was to sample vintages from previous years. Perhaps it would have been an insult to refuse this step in the procedure, for Granddaddy was definitely not a drinking man.

However it came about, I was too young to know, but Granddaddy came home slightly inebriated. Nannie had been busy baking cream pies for next day's Sunday company. She placed the pies to cool on a bench that sat close to the cookstove.

Enter Granddaddy who didn't feel well and needed to sit down. The closest thing at hand was the bench by the range. And yes, Granddaddy sat on one of the cream pies! I recall that Nannie was a mite put out. I believe the next year when Granddaddy did his neighborly duty by Jojo, he was very careful about the tasting.

Our very first neighbors when we moved to Nail Farm were Lena, whom I have already introduced, Addie, and Roy. We would never have survived without their help over the years, Addie with the children and Roy with many of our crops. Roy and his trusty shovel were by- words in our experience. More than once he had to shovel my car out of a ditch. I thought he knew how to do just about anything.

One time when the children were small and Edwin worked at night, we came home and found a strange man lying in the field next to our yard. Not slowing down, I went hightailing up the road to get Roy. Soon as I told him our problem, he got in the car and came home with us. We all hurried into the house, Roy locking the door behind us while I quickly called the police.

The police came, identified the fellow who was drunk, and hauled him off to jail. Not knowing he was harmless, I recall the confidence I felt that Roy would protect us, even though he was getting on in years.

The roll call in my recollection unfurls others who came and went on our road. We were so honored when we were invited to celebrate the 50th wedding anniversary of the wonderful old couple whose land adjoined ours. Reuben, Anne, Murray, Allen and Sherry, Lourene and Larry, Margaret and Jim, the young Hammock couple—all with whom we shared the give and take of neighbors. Today there are Peter and Ruth, who have helped me with many and varied things.

Sandi and Harold bought the place next to us thirty-something years ago. They were the personification of good neighbors. We helped each other through family crises, rejoiced in the good times, and wept with the sad. They were young, vibrant and full of energy. We could count on them in any situation and we gave evidence of the same loyalty to them. I thought they would be here to help tie up our loose ends. It doesn't seem possible that they didn't live long after Edwin.

Then there was Sims, who never lived close to us, but I use his example here because he is the best definition of a neighbor. He and Edwin had known each other a long time. He came by one day to order some hay. As they talked Edwin told him from which bay in the barn to get the hay. If we weren't at home, he could load it himself. Sims agreed that he would do that, laughed and added, "If anybody asks what I'm doing here, I'll just tell them I'm your brother." Edwin told him that would be fine and they shook hands on it, Edwin's tanned white one and Sims ebony one. Neighbor and brother are closely related. It doesn't matter what color we are, or where we hail from. Anyway, they were spiritual brothers.

James, a neighbor across town, and Edwin had worked together many years ago, and he helped out with farm work sometimes when Edwin needed an extra man. James was the one who summoned Edwin from the field when Wayne broke his arm. The little guy, straining to get high enough to see his daddy in the field with the new corn picker, fell off the back stoop.

In my memory book I see James and Edwin loading truck loads of watermelon from the field and gathering fresh corn for customers. It made the work go quicker when you had someone to laugh with. James was always there when we needed him, interwoven into our lives and ours with his. After Edwin's death James helped me with numerous outdoor tasks.

Bill and Linda are neighbors just down the road. Linda has the most generous heart of anybody I know. Although she was a full time police officer, she helped me by sitting with Mama on weekend nights.

One day Brenda decided the dead tree trunk which stood at our front drive was dead enough to be separated from its roots. She and I hooked a chain around the tree and the other end to the tractor. Bill was going by and stopped to keep us from killing ourselves. He fastened one chain to his pickup so when Brenda powered up the tractor with a mighty pull the tree wouldn't fall over and hit her in the head. It worked! Pulled off nice and easy and only whacked the tractor roof a little, but it wasn't Brenda's head.

That's the way Bill is. When he drives by I feel secure that if anything were wrong Bill would notice and do something about it, as he has already done many times.

A neighbor of my aunt's, who long ago purchased a tract of land from her, walked far more than the second mile to help me after my husband was gone. He and Edwin had once worked together and for years he had gotten corn from our plentiful fields. That next year when I struggled alone with the planters getting the corn into the ground Mr. Thompson came to my rescue. Not content merely to show me how, he followed on foot every inch those planters turned for several rows to adjust them just right.

Our newest neighbor is Steven. He helped us after the barn fire and is always quick to tell me that if I ever need him just to call.

I would like to add to the definition that a neighbor is someone who shares with you the daily living, the joys and woes, the hard times, the good times, who is indeed a brother, and with them you share the same.

"You have said, Lord, that a neighbor is one who stops to help another when there is need. Thank You for those who have done unto us what You have commanded. They have given us many boosts up the hills we've had to climb on the Emmaus Road."

Chapter 47
Keys

My husband was a man of many talents. His nature was positive, forever looking for the best of things. Whereas I on the other hand, was surely born negative. My premise was: imagine the worst, and when it isn't you get a pleasant surprise.

On occasion I would get a little annoyed at how he seemed to know things were going to be all right. For example, our teenage daughter had been loading firewood onto the pickup. Later that afternoon she discovered she had lost her turquoise pendant. The silver chain still hung around her neck, but the tiny emblem was gone. She was especially distressed since it had been a Christmas gift.

She and I returned to the woods in a half-hearted effort at finding it. Certainly, a piece of jewelry smaller than a dime would be like finding a needle in a haystack. We were so sure we wouldn't succeed, we didn't.

When her daddy came home and I relayed the loss to him he said,"Let's go down there and get it," like it was a done deal.

That cheerful confidence again! I argued, "It's absolutely useless. We've already looked and looked." He wouldn't accept the 'we won't find it' excuse, so once again I trailed along behind him to the woods.

We scratched among the leaves and chips as we had done before while I kept thinking, "What a waste of my time." Just then I looked down at my feet and there it lay on a large brown leaf! My husband grinned, "I just felt like we'd find it when we came to look."

I began to wonder—just how much does attitude play in our successes? I thought about what Jesus said concerning the search for a lost coin. He called it a diligent search. Apparently, it is important to do a search like we believe we will find it. Is that the key?

On our sitting room wall hang three large warded keys which were used regularly when our farm was the family plantation. Although we haven't used them in years, they would still fit a couple of locks in the old barn until it burned in 2003.

In appearance there is little difference between the keys. They look as if they might open the same doors. But they wouldn't. I could never remember which were the right ones and had to try each one to seek the proper fit.

Sometimes our problems are much like locked doors that we are unable to unlock. We try one solution, and then another. Nothing seems to work. There appears no way out of our dilemma.

That's when someone could remind us that there is a key to every door. If one doesn't fit, we try another. If we should keep trying, by trial and error we might eventually find the proper key to our problem.

It occurred to me then how the Christian has a better way. Jesus did not leave us to muddle alone, trying one solution and then another. He sent Someone in His place, the Holy Spirit, to guide us.

I am not blessed with the inborn confidence and positiveness that Edwin had but I discovered I could put into practice an attitude of sincere seeking and asking which can be the key to opening doors. If it is Jesus who turns the lock, we can be sure it's the right entrance for us and not a forced entry.

Even in the final weeks of his life, my husband was the uplifter. He is the one who helped us feel better. When he relinquished himself to God's timing, his natural positivism tried to tell me it was going to be all right, that I was going to be all right. I couldn't begin to perceive how it could possibly be, but in time I was able to understand that with Jesus as the Keeper of my life's keys I would not be walking down the road alone.

✺ঔৣ৵✺

"So many times, I find myself standing at locked doors of indecision. It has been hard to continue my journey without my lifetime traveler. But when I truly seek Your answers, Lord, and not my own, You hand me the proper key."

Chapter 48
A Salute to the Captain

The crowd was beginning to disperse. People who had not seen each other in some time embraced, and said their goodbyes. It was a sad time. Our friend, Louise, had just been laid to rest in the cemetery on the hill. I looked back for my grown children when I realized they had one last thing to do.

Previously, at some point in their lives when Louise had been put in charge by them and herself to handle a situation which required decisions, they "commissioned" her Captain. They gave her the respect and honor of being the Captain in Charge.

It was a fitting title. She was one of those people who could get things organized, running smoothly, and ready to tackle the next project with what appeared to be little effort.

Now I watched as they stood at attention with fingers raised to their brow in final salute. It didn't matter to them what other people thought. Louise had been part of their lives ever since they had entered this world. It brought further tears to my eyes for I was biding a final farewell to one of those special friends who is always there for you.

Pete and Louise had been our friends for almost as long as

Edwin and I were married, but it goes back even farther than that. Pete's mother and Edwin's grandmother had been neighbors and friends all their lives.

When Edwin's daddy died, it was Pete who took days off from his own job to help Edwin harvest the grain crop. It was Pete who helped Edwin get our house in shape to move into when Wayne was a baby.

It was Louise and Pete who helped us get Aunt Berta home from the hospital and into her own home before her death. They were always there when we had a great need.

After Pete was gone, their daughter Ramona built a bookstore. Edwin helped her complete the interior. It became an important and joyful task for him to finish the walls and build the bookshelves, for much of his carpentry knowledge had come from Pete, a master carpenter. In repaying a debt to a friend by helping his daughter, I believe Edwin liked to think that Pete's hand joined his on the hammer.

One night after Edwin had been in surgery for hours I left him in intensive care and came home to tend to our animals. A terrible storm had raged all afternoon. When I left the hospital, lightning made jagged slashes across the sky and the rain came down in blinding sheets.

At home I hurried into the house thankful we still had electricity but the phone was dead. What was I to do? I couldn't stay here without a phone in case the hospital called.

Louise knew I was on my way home. When she couldn't get through by telephone, she insisted Ramona drive her down to see if I was all right.

Just as I was about to fall apart they drove into the yard. Seldom have I been more thankful to see anyone. It was such a comfort that they waited while I ran to feed the horse and the other animals. About then the phone rang—service was restored.

It was as if Louise had brought peace and a sense of order with her. She let me talk about my fear, absorbing it with her love and concern. I shall never forget that stormy, anxious night and how comforted and supported I was by friends.

When I would get discouraged over a rejection of something I had written, Louise would bolster me up. She refused to let me give up on what she felt was my calling. Even if we were not together, she would say, "Read it to me over the phone." When I did, it often helped iron out the wrinkles and it would become clearer.

Louise simply would not let me give up on a mystery I was writing for young people. She was gone before it was published, but at my first book signing I know if it was at all possible she was looking on with pride and joy for me each time I wrote my name in the book, "The Summer of Anchor's Mystery."

Sometimes now when I get bogged down and sit staring at the computer screen I get a punch from behind. I tell myself it's only a mental punch but I'm not so sure.

Not long ago I received a book on writing that I had not ordered. I sat down to look it over before packaging it up to return it to the post office. Interested that it contained suggestions and pointers that were definite solutions to some writing problems I had, I realized it was just what I needed to get me fired up again.

Ramona and I laughed and said Louise ordered the exact copy required. Of course, it's just a joke. But I'm not so sure.

⁂

"How precious are the friends You connect us with in this life, Father, those who make us better people and refuse to allow us to give up on ourselves. Louise was a great companion on this Emmaus Road. I praise You, Lord, for the supports and prompts You encouraged her to give."

Chapter 49
Cousins Removed

She called me Aunt Clara, which deeply touched me. I thought I should explain our real blood relationship so as not to confuse family, but I don't think she was one bit interested. Nonetheless, I wanted her to know how wonderful her great-great-grandparents had been.

It went back to a promise her great-great-grandmother had made to my grandmother. They were first cousins. My grandmother's dying request was that her cousin raise my mother. Somehow when the time came, my mama got lost in the shuffle and was sent to an orphanage. Mama was eight years old when Nannie eventually located her and took her home. Mama and Nannie were first cousins once removed.

Nannie and Granddaddy had one daughter. She and my mother were second cousins. The children of that daughter and Mama were second cousins once removed. Those children and I are third cousins. Then their children and my children are fourth cousins and the children of my third cousins and I are third cousins once removed.

By then I knew I had completely lost my young third cousin

once removed, and not sure but that I had lost me too. The point is: the same blood does run through our veins and occasionally we see some of the same genes pop up.

My third cousins are the brother and sisters I never had, and we have always been extremely close. We grew up together, sometimes even living in the same house.

I looked up the word family. Will Durant called it the "nucleus of civilization". Carson McCullers called it "the we of me." I like that one. Being part of a family group gave me a stability I would not have had if Mama and I were always alone. I had back-up when I needed it.

Present day we hear a lot about the extended family, the steps and in-laws. Back then those under Nannie and Granddaddy's roof were a varied conglomerate. It's a good thing the house was big.

Besides Nannie and Granddaddy there was Mama and me after Daddy died, Mary, one of Nannie's nieces, Jack, an unrelated army sergeant of World War I, and sometimes Nannie's mother. At various times during the depression Reba, the daughter, and her husband, Nelson, also lived there with their children, my third cousins.

The first cousins and the second cousins are all gone now. All we have of the house on the hill is memories.

Clarene is the only one of us who lives within a few miles of it. A few years ago I flew to Ohio to visit and also, I think, to find something from the past I could touch base with again. I really didn't understand it myself, except that after my husband died I sort of lost my identity. I wasn't a daughter anymore, or a daughter-in-law, or a niece. Now I wasn't a wife. Widow is such a sad word I couldn't come to terms with it. I didn't know me anymore. It seemed all the we's were gone.

The day after I arrived in Ohio, we climbed into Clarene's car and began our journey, into the past and yet not. The route we took was overwhelmingly present-day with all the shifts and changes. Clarene reminisced while I frantically searched for something familiar which might satisfy my memory trip into the past.

Always before when I returned to Ohio I could close my eyes and know I was there from the smell of greenery—alfalfa perhaps. This time the fragrance didn't come to me. Had so much construction taken the place of all the farms?

As Clarene drove through the main street of Milford I was pleased to see much of it remained the same. On Round Bottom Road I recognized the spot above the Little Miami River where our school bus made its turnaround to head back toward Newtown, our school district. When we turned onto Mount Carmel Road I was happy to see a familiar farm house. Another turn put us on Broadwell, where we had all lived in the house on the hill.

I was distressed that not one thing—the beds of iris, nor roses, the lilac bushes, nor any tree—remained of the home yard. The hillside had been completely removed. In place of the house sprawled a huge manufacturing plant. Not one remnant was left of the great barn across the road where Jack's last saddle horse, Bess, had died.

A little farther we crossed railroad tracks that had lain there forever. In my mind's eye I could see Granddaddy on the hill at the house, hands folded behind his back, counting the rail cars when the freights went by.

At the other end of Broadwell we turned once more onto Round Bottom. The little grocery seemed to be in business. It was the only store closer than Newtown. Sometimes Nannie would send me on my pony to pick up something she needed.

In Newtown we drove onto the school street where we both

had attended primary school. Clarene told me it is no longer the public school. I longed to walk into the main hall to see if the wide staircase was still there. From third grade through sixth the big kids were in classrooms upstairs. We were only permitted to use the front stairway each morning upon arriving and afternoon upon leaving.

Continuing on down the street, we saw the shop which held in one alcove a small lending library where Nannie and I felt privileged to get books, then the post office and next door the house where Mama lived during World War II. Both buildings now held a flea market.

Clarene parked the car and we got out. She busied herself looking at some baskets, while I wandered into the yard where my mother had lived so many years ago. I never really lived in the house but I had spent a whole summer there with Mama. As part of the business it was now open to the public so I stepped inside the front room. I felt I would burst with emotion. It was the same! It had barely changed. It seemed I was also inside the past! It was so familiar I thought surely Mama would be in the next room.

My inner vision could "see" her cook stove in the kitchen, and the big leather chair in front of the window where I would sit to read letters from Edwin, who was serving in the armed forces in Japan. I could see the beautiful library table in its place before the double windows, the big warm burner that warmed the house in winter, the lovely lawyer's book case with the glass doors. From the window my gaze focused on the back yard once filled with Mama's flowers. Portions of the fence were left standing.

Clarene knew the store's proprietor and they were busy discussing mutual friends. Grateful for a few moments alone, I thought of the long road Mama and I traveled since the time she lived in this house. Tears began to silently slide down my face.

I asked myself why I needed to make this trip. I didn't

understand it, but it was something I had to do. Was it going home again, a return to young promises the future held, the dreams we have, the hopes?

It was not wrenching grief I experienced, for this particular house held little meaning for me. Not like "being home again", yet there was joy in touching familiar walls and door facings. It was as if the tears in that house washed something out.

Those brief moments within the walls of a youthful summer set something free in me. I had not lost my identity; I was the same me God had created. Perhaps I just needed to go back and touch base with beginnings.

I would always be my mother's daughter, and nothing could take away from me the lifetime Edwin and I had shared. My role may have shifted a bit, but what Edwin had told me when he was dying was true. Something remained for me to do, and to be.

While Clarene and I finished our trek along paths we had traveled growing up, I was reminded of how much we share memory-wise and blood-wise. It was one of her granddaughters to whom I tried to explain the cousin relationship. It is to that generation—the children of Clarene, her sister Helen, and brother Jerry that I am third cousin once removed.

Nothing can change that. It is the we of me.

⁂

"Father God, I praise Your wonderful plan for families, for the love that flows through the blood lines of generations. I thank You especially for these cousins and their spouses, Gene, Harold, and Jeanie, who have made this journey so much more fulfilling and complete, and helped me to belong. My gratitude spills over to You, Lord Jesus, who walks with us."

Chapter 50
Mama's Gift

With an identifying squeak of saddle and the smell of horse and leather, I can feel the big animal move beneath me. But I am not alone. My mother, a skilled horsewoman sits behind me, one arm encircling my middle, the reins in her efficient other hand.

Many decades have passed since this early childhood memory which remains one of my clearest concerning my mother. Its reminder is of her supporting me from behind and encircling me with her love, as she always did even in her sunset years when the days were sometimes cloudy with forgetfulness.

I had not heard the term, "horse whisperer" until a few years ago. I believe Mama had that gift, or something very close to it. She was wonderful with all animals but she and horses had a particular bond. She could calm the most frightened just by speaking to them and laying her hand on them. She could bind up slashed wounds, while they whickered soft sounds like children whimpering at soothing touches. When she rode they would respond to her every command. It upset Nannie that Mama would jump her horse over the farm gates instead of opening them.

Now I realized that at eighty six she had not lost the ability to communicate with horses. The farm adjoining her yard held several of the beautiful animals, who would hang over the fence bumping each other vying for attention when she would go out to talk to them.

I became slightly uneasy when one day she announced, "After supper I'm going to take a ride if I can find my saddle." The saddle was something else that was, "lost in the barn." I knew she would not find the saddle, and the horses were not hers, and she probably would forget it. But I still warned the sitter. Strong minded and determined by nature, Mama usually accomplished what she put her mind to.

She was active and able for her age and not afraid of anything in this life except snakes. At least she said she feared them. I much doubted it for she would ramble around in the woods that surrounded her house and hunt them with a pitchfork. Pity any poor snake that she dug out with that weapon. If I fear something I will at all cost avoid it, not seek it out. Mama's premise was to get rid of the fear by eliminating the object.

On occasion when she tried my patience, I envied my peers who had gentlewomen for mothers. Those who were satisfied to sit quietly and knit, or look at television. At least you knew where they were. The more our roles reversed with me as the reluctant mother figure, the more I remembered the stories Nannie used to tell about Mama's childhood. I don't know why we assume a little age changes people all that much for it often doesn't.

Mama had always been good at weaving a tale. Age seemed to not only confuse one with the other, but enabled her to embellish and prevaricate with colorful twists and turns. I was horrified at some things she told people. Even those who knew us well probably began to wonder a great deal about this family. Sometimes I wondered myself.

All the women in my life have been strong women—Nannie, Aunt Berta, even my genteel grandmother, and then Mama. Their standards would never allow me to take the weak way out.

I had a pony but I'd never owned a bicycle and I longed to know how to ride. The neighbor boys rode theirs into our yard. When they let me try I promptly fell off. My impulse was to go to my room, fling myself across the bed and cry. Not with Mama around, I didn't. She made me get back on that bike, steadied me briefly until I got a good start and then let me go. She wouldn't let me give up, and she knew when to let go.

After Mama was gone, to fill some of the void I experienced at her leaving I settled down to write "The Summer of Anchor's Mystery". Because of her, I chose a horse farm as the setting and grieved that she missed helping me with it.

However, when I think about it, she had done that with the examples of courage and fortitude she provided each day of her life. She always encircled me with her love; perhaps that is why the memory of sitting a horse with her strength behind me is so vivid. She knew when to help, and when to let go. And, perhaps it is better to rout out what we fear and eliminate it.

※ЖСЖ※

"I am eternally grateful for the strong women in my life. Their examples set a pattern that has stayed with me even though all of them have left this sphere. I appreciate Mama's gifts and praise You, Lord Jesus, for helping us over the rough patches of the road when all was not smooth traveling."

Chapter 51
Anchor's Mystery

When our children were young their great-uncle Troy would entertain them with stories about their great-great grandfather— of the War Between the States era—who had, in fact, been a Confederate soldier.

I would listen enthralled, and would jot down ideas for what I dreamed could one day be a good story if I could just get around to writing it. Every day when the dogs and I would take our walk through wood paths and across field terraces, I would think of another idea for a possible chapter. When I'd get to the house, I'd pull out my notebook and scribble it down.

Great Grandfather Nail's time here was long before I came upon the scene. Somehow living in his house, and working in his fields and barns, I feel a strong connection to him and to his bachelor sons who lived here until their deaths.

The years scooted by and it wasn't until my children were long grown that I finally decided I didn't have forever on this planet. While I had written other things, mostly inspirational articles, I had not pursued my dream of the juvenile mystery.

Then Mama died and I desperately needed a new avenue to

run down. If I ever intended to make those notes into a story, I had better begin. I would use a horse farm as the setting. It would help me feel closer to her and the memory of her gift with horses.

However, when I got out the notes I had created, there didn't appear to be nearly enough for a book manuscript. I remember telling God I was disappointed in myself. Were all those years of inner excitement about it only a fantasy?

Make a beginning. The impression in my mind was strong to make a beginning. I began with what I had for the first chapter. The next one came easier. Half way through the book I wrote the final chapter and then went back to fill in those in between. And so it flowed. Better still, it poured out of me. I could hardly type fast enough. Ideas came to my mind that amazed even me. I neglected my husband, I put off feeding the animals, I cooked quick meals and washed only the clothes we needed right then.

The characters in the story have much the same personality of my children at that age. Once a year we would journey to visit Ohio kin. Our kids would jump out of the car and they and their cousins would pick up as if they had left off the previous day instead of the previous year. Never any awkward re-acquaintance, same as in the book.

I finished the first draft. About that time, doubt came in swift and strong. Had it not been for my friend Louise, who absolutely wouldn't allow me to give up, I would never have done the rewrite. She more than encouraged. She coerced.

I finished it and mailed it to a few publishers. When it would return unaccepted, I went back to my old way. I'd stick it away in my file cabinet. At least it was an improvement over a sock drawer or the freezer, where I had exiled rejected manuscripts in the past.

Eventually I found a publisher who was willing to give me a chance. With the invaluable aid of my son, who is great at editing and a computer specialist to boot, the final draft was ready. In the spring of 2003 "The Summer of Anchor's Mystery" was accepted by Publish America, and came out one year later.

It was an exciting time, yet with a touch of sadness. My mother could have helped me with the horse theme, but I had waited too long. Louise would have been ecstatic; she had looked forward to its publication. But Louise had also died. I waited too long.

I couldn't change what I had done, or not done. But it made me more mindful of not putting off important things. I discovered first-hand, it can be too late.

I like to think that Mama and Louise are still cheering me on. In fact, the day of my first book signing at Pleasant Hill Books I sensed their strong presence. While it may have been my imagination, it made me feel better anyway. Or perhaps, it was just the joy of the day.

Pleasant Hill Books is owned by Ramona, Louise's daughter. It was a special day for me and for my children, although butterflies were fluttering in my stomach. Ramona placed a fancy chair before the signing table. She prepared lovely refreshments to serve potential customers. Brenda had attractively displayed the books. Wayne stood by to hold me up. Everything was ready. What if nobody comes?

They came. They began to trickle in. Then, if you looked down the country road you could see a long line of cars rounding the curve and heading up the hill to the book store. One after the other. Wonderful people who came to support me! My friends, Ramona's friends, people I'd never seen before. Lovely people! I was overwhelmed. At that first signing, I sold sixty-six books.

My cup ran over. I felt I had been anointed with oil, and surely goodness and mercy attended that lovely spring day. As to high points in my life, it ranked with my wedding and the birth of my children.

It was an extraordinary gift from God. With only a few ideas for it, once I was obedient and began to write, He gave me the rest. I felt I had put it off too long; He had a different time schedule. It is fantastic to perceive He is in control of us, our interests, our dreams—even a juvenile mystery story, and our eventuality.

"You know the inner workings of all that I am and what makes me who I am, for You made me. Wondrous God, Helper and Creator, thank You for small successes along the road. Thank You for a joyful story that I wrote as You gave, and thank You for the years with Uncle Troy who spun a fine tale as we traveled along."

Chapter 52
The Power of Prayer

Wayne, my son, who once had difficulty stepping over the clods of plowed earth, can now easily step over the chunks in his path. However, as with all of us, while he may sporadically find the way to be smooth and easily traversed, inevitably the chunks and obstacles return. It's the way of life.

After Mama passed away I had for a time rented her house and acreage. Then when Edwin knew he was soon to leave us, he suggested I sell it. The following winter when Wayne was here for Christmas, he helped me prepare the house and parcel of land for sale. Strangely, when I expected to sign the final papers it didn't materialize. A block seemed to be in front of the decision so I waited, uncertain as to why.

The next year Wayne called to say he would like to move from Maryland into his grandmother's house. I never dreamed he would come back to this area, although it has been an immeasurable blessing for me.

Wayne's very existence is a constant reminder to me of my first real experience with believing prayer. Edwin and I had been married for six years and still had no joyous news to announce. At first it was okay; we needed to get used to each other. Eventually, we began to anticipate the patter of little feet. Yet that hope seemed to be diminishing.

Having been a Christian for many years I was familiar with prayer, mostly the God-bless type. However, I don't think I ever approached God with real soul wrenching petition. I can recall thinking, "Well, I'll ask God about this, but I doubt it will be of much help." My unbelief firmly decided we were not to have a child.

In my ignorance I had placed three blocks in my path to answered prayer. Shallowness, doubt, and second-guessing God. With my shallow praying I was not only doubting God's power, I predetermined what His answer would be. I closed the window through which any blessing could come.

Then one morning alone in our bedroom reading my Bible, I came across the passage of Scripture from Mark where it says, "That whosoever shall say unto this mountain, be thou removed, and shall not doubt in his heart, but shall believe that those things which he saith shall come to pass; he shall have whatsoever he saith" (Mark 11:23 KJV).

I heard the words of Jesus echoing down the tunnels of time to my present day and dilemma where he said, "What things soever you desire, when you pray, believe that you receive them and you shall have them" (Mark 11:24 KJV).

From His Holy Word Jesus was speaking to me personally, providing me with instruction as how to remove the mountain, which I had with blind precision molded in my own path. A light came on! Through this passage in Mark's gospel the Holy Spirit opened my mind and heart to receiving truth.

Then I was enabled to pray truly seeking, with humility and profound belief in the power of the Lord Jesus to answer the deepest desire my heart had ever sought. My part was to believe it was possible, and leave the rest to Him.

I shall never forget that day. When the first buds were appearing and wild geese were flying northward, winter was ending in my soul. I walked outside and at the corner of the house the pear tree, which the day before was as barren as I, was completely covered in white blossoms. The confirmation of new life that spring brings us every year!

Rising out of the very depths of knowing and quite beyond mere feeling, came the positive assurance that my plea would be answered. It was the first time my inner listening heard God speak directly to me, but clearly I received the words. "By the time spring awakens next year, you will have borne a child." I never allowed myself to doubt it and belief brought proof. Wayne was the child, who was born just prior to the pear tree's annual announcement of another spring.

He brought us much joy as a little guy and a bit of hair tearing as a teen. It was wonderful when he passed the age where we, his parents, became literate people again. Wayne is a perfectionist in all he does, from his gourmet cooking to his computer specialty. We laugh with admiration and say that he can fix our computers over the telephone.

When he lived at home he had to help with all the farm chores. He became a little more knowledgeable about machinery and how it works than his sister and I. When the three of us were left to manage what once was a thriving farm, none of us felt qualified to handle all it entailed. Even though we aren't now actually farming, we plant a big garden and several corn patches, and keep the brush and weeds mowed.

It was Wayne who came up with the idea that three of us together could at least make up one farm-wise brain. What one didn't know, couldn't do, or could think of maybe the other two would. So that is the premise we have used to deal with what the man of the family left us. It has worked pretty well. It has given us many laughs, which is another thing I appreciate about this son. He has a great sense of humor.

Like a lot of people, one thing he has not discovered is the gift that believing prayer can be to us. First, we have to believe in God who, through His Son Jesus, grants this gift.

Early, I accepted what Jesus came to do for any who would acknowledge Him and by faith ask Him into their heart. While I knew Him personally, I had not traveled deeply enough in my walk with Him to comprehend the gift that was mine for the asking — the gift of prayer. Every time I look at my son I am reminded of the moment when truth came through bright and clear as the spring day when I received the promise of this child.

Only then did I finally understand what prayer really is — it's the reality of approaching God. It contains the same power which God used to raise Jesus from death. Because I believe and embrace that act, I have access to the power of prayer, as do all believers as long as what we ask can be in the permissible will of God.

Prayer is His gift to those who follow Him, one which we never use up, and contains all the potential our belief will permit it.

⁂

"That certain spring day was the beginning of a new level in my walk with You, Lord Jesus. It is marked in my inner being, strong and indelible. I praise You for the answer to my specific entreaty even before the tiny inception of life had begun."

Chapter 53
Love Letters

Noting the dust that roiled up as I applied dust cloth and vacuum, I moved some furniture out from the wall to clean under and behind it. When I pulled open one of the drawers I saw the bundle of letters. Dated every few days apart, they were stamped with the years 1945 through '46. Love letters from a soldier.

I placed them in order according to dates on the envelopes, some with APO addresses, some stateside, all written during World War II and the occupation afterwards. I sat down to read them, and was transported back to the time when I was fourteen and fifteen years old. I could almost feel the same girlish thrill I received when the mailbox held one with my name on it.

They were letters from my husband. Although it would be several years until that relationship came to pass, he was already telling me that I was the love of his life and we would spend our life together.

It took me several hours and parts of two days to read them. It set a strange mood, almost like I was getting reacquainted with the young soldier who wrote them. He was only eighteen and nineteen, away from home for the first time and cast into a scary time of learning how to make war, how to kill the enemy before they killed you.

I could sense he would rather be anywhere else, but mostly home! You could feel his growth, even a certain hardening of the inner person as time passed. Gradually an acceptance came as he set himself to the task before him, making the best he could of the situation at hand. Upon his return after more than a year on foreign soil, he was not the same boy who had marched away. Like many others, those things he saw and lived added extra years to his life.

After all this time I still find it amazing how one thing never changed, and that was his love for me. In one of the letters he mentioned those strong first feelings. A group of us were playing baseball in the pasture of one of our friends when we first met. I was thirteen and he was seventeen. Of course, I wasn't allowed to date and was not particularly interested in him anyway. He was too old. Also, he was part family. While not related to me, he was Uncle Bob's nephew. Uncle Bob was my Aunt Berta's husband.

The day after I'd read all the letters, our children came by. I was in a pensive mood thinking about the time warp the letters had placed me in. It was almost a shock to realize these middle aged people were our children. Where on earth had the years gone?

They were good years. Mountains to climb, rivers to forge, valleys to cross but we did it together for the forty-seven and a half years we were granted. Edwin was right. We had spent most of our life together. It just went too quickly.

While reading the young declaration of his love for me, I relived the separation the distance placed on us. Even so, there was always the underlying hope that, God willing, he would return. Even with the thousands of miles between us, he was still in this world. It gave me a jolt to return to the present moment when I realized anew he had moved beyond this world as we know it.

Like many, I wish I could go back and relive some of those years, maybe make better choices of how time was spent. It sharpens my awareness of making the most of each experience, of committing myself to walking the Emmaus Road more fully cognizant of the Presence of Jesus, who makes it all possible, as we journey onward.

❧❦❧

"Thank You, God, for those years with my lifetime mate, and for the love which surrounded me. The bonds of that love still embrace me, and the letters remind me how death did not end my love for him, nor his for me."

Chapter 54
Cotton

In January 1955 we moved into our great-grandparents' house on the farm that had long been in my husband's family. A simple move of household furnishings it was not. When a whole farm is relocated all the mechanical equipment, seed, hay, fertilizer, cattle, chickens, hogs, right down to the cats and dogs have to be hauled to the new place. It took several days with a lot of helpers.

That year cotton was expected to bring a good market price. Except for the pasture, the orchard, and our garden plot it seemed a good plan to use all the acreage allotment the government permitted us for cotton. Our goal took in not only our farm, but great Uncle Charlie's acreage and some rented land on another farm. Acres and acres of cotton. My husband did all the plowing and planting, hired day laborers for the hoeing and chopping, and got through the summer of arsenic spraying to keep the boll weevils at bay.

Then, in order to supplement our financial need until the harvest, Edwin went to work for a manufacturing company in town. Now it was my turn. In order to get the day laborers required for the cotton gathering, you had to be out early to pick up those who were ready to work in your fields. Only a few had their own transportation. Word got around that you needed day labor and soon you could pick them up at designated points each morning.

Our first born was just a toddler, so I let him sleep as long as possible and then would tuck him, pajama-clad, under my arm and head for the car. There I would settle him beside me with his bottle. With no time to lose I have to admit that sometimes my foot was a bit heavy on the pedal, but I prided myself on getting workers to the field about the time the sun cracked the horizon.

The older matrons criticized me sometimes rather sharply about bringing my baby out so early, in his pajamas at that, but what was I to do? I had no one at home to tend him. Besides, he seemed to thrive on it and made lots of friends with the men and women I trucked to and fro from field to field and home again.

There was one fly in the ointment. One older gentleman tried my patience beyond endurance by never being ready when I arrived in his yard. Invariably he would still be eating breakfast and seemed to take pleasure that he made me cool my motor while he finished, something I knew he would never do to my husband. When he would finally be ready to leave, I would have to speed up more than usual to get them all to the field by what they considered a decent hour.

One day at paying time, he remarked to my husband that it was a good thing his wife not been born in horse and buggy days. When Edwin asked him why, he said, "Because she'd a run many a good horse to death." I have to admit it smarted a bit, but it didn't cause me to mend my waywardness.

When Edwin had to work the evening shift, it was up to me to take the big truck to the different fields at weighing up time and for loading the cotton onto the truck.

Most pickers provided their own pick-sack which was a long

cloth bag, sometimes a heavy flour sack but more often a croker sack which had a shoulder strap sewn to it. All day long the pickers pulled cotton from the sticky burrs and placed it in their sacks. It was a back breaking, finger sticking task. When their sack got full they dumped the cotton out onto a cotton sheet, usually made from the same material and provided by the planter. Each picker had his or her own sheet. At day's end the four corners were brought together and tied. A hook from a steelyard was slipped over a pole or stick held by two people. The sheet full of cotton was picked up by another hook on the balance scale and the weight was written down for each cotton bundle.

I received only one complaint during weighing-up time. A grandmother protested that she'd never had a woman weigh up her cotton. However, when it occurred to her that without it she would not receive her pay I never heard that grumble again. I was always careful that two of the male pickers checked the weight as well.

When the truck was full to overflowing with bolls and bolls of white, seed stuffed cotton it was driven to the cotton gin where they de-seeded, de-linted, blended, mashed, and did whatever else they did to it before squashing it into huge bales. Cotton and fall seemed to go together and I can still close my eyes and savor the scents of the cotton harvest.

While cotton is presently grown in many places, it is mostly a thing of the past in our area. Today's children will never experience that time in history, the pages having long turned to another chapter. There is sad nostalgia in realizing that the beautiful fields once white with harvest are now covered in plank and brick and mortar.

It is then I remember the fields are, as Jesus said, "white under harvest," this time with souls who need Him. I ask myself if I will be as faithful with those fields as I was with our cotton acres.

As I relive that time in these pages I am truly in awe of the strength that was given me to pull both sides of the yoke when my husband had to be elsewhere. That's what teams are all about, and while it is not easy, a certain satisfaction comes from knowing you did your part to the best of your ability.

I am strongly reminded where the strength and ability come from, and of how God gives what you need at the precise time of need.

Gradually we cut back our cotton production, which was a great relief to Uncle Charlie, who thought it was beyond the proper thing for a lady. Driving a truck and weighing up cotton was not what he believed the females in his family should be doing.

❦

"Father, when I recall that period of my life it is almost as if I see someone else and it is not me at all. Then I feel my young son tucked under my arm as I head for the car in the crisp early morning. We are on our way to another day in another time with hard-working faithful people who shared the toil of honest labor. I thank you for those who walked with us along that dusty portion of our road."

Chapter 55
Irrevocable Ties

In the South we have been much criticized and maligned because our ancestors once owned slaves. As a product of the South as well as north of the Mason-Dixon line, I have seen both sides of the black-white issue.

It is true my southern great-grandparents had slaves. I am not proud of the fact, nor am I in any way responsible for their actions. The premise about our generation paying for the sins of our fathers makes about as much sense to me as suing a neighbor just because he is of Japanese descent, and thus somehow responsible for Japan's role in World War II.

Nothing was right about slavery. I am totally opposed to anything that smacks of one human being enslaving another for any purpose whatsoever, so do not misunderstand what I am about to say.

Even with all its wrongness, there is something that newer generations, as well as those from other parts of our country, do not understand about the relationships that existed pre-Civil War which carried over into the tenant-landowner period of the South after the war.

While none of us today were present, much has been chronicled from those in the past who were. Although I can write only from the perspective of my family, I have heard similar testimony from many others.

I am aware that certain landowners treated their slaves in the worst possible way. However, it was not true in every case. After they were freed, a number returned to the farms and the families who had once housed and fed them. I know it is said they didn't have much choice for all they knew was plantation life, which is a legitimate point. Yet in many cases, for whatever reasons, they simply went home. It was familiar and became a way of survival for both the landowner and the newly freed.

In reality without thought or plan the pattern followed a practice that has existed since mankind has inhabited this earth— the law of symbiosis. Separate they were ineffectual, but together they would be the aid the other required. In this case, the land owner could not alone work the large tracts of farmland, and the laborer needed a place to live with the basic necessities of life. Their need for each other was mutual, and so began another chapter in our history.

When the Yankees marched into Georgia, seized Atlanta and headed toward Henry County, white males who were old and infirm were killed or taken prisoner. If there was enough warning some of them concealed themselves. My great-grandfather, a cripple, was one of those. He had gone to his farm on the outskirts of town to hide a cow in a briar thicket, hoping to save the milk supply for the little children of his household. When word reached him that a Federal unit had reached McDonough, he and an elderly gentleman sought safety in an old dry well.

The Yankee troops lingered and headquartered in McDonough which meant the men had to stay hidden for some time. The Mammy to Great-Grandpa's children would smuggle food in her apron, walk by the hiding place, and drop it so the men would not starve. Would she have done this if she had been mistreated? It would have been easier to report them.

A child born into slavery on my great-grandparents farm during the war never broke his tie with my family. Although he was very old, when I was a teen he still worked occasionally for Aunt Berta. The love they had for each other was a precious thing to behold. To my aunt this fine old gentleman was family as much as her flesh and blood. Theirs was a special bond.

Aunt Berta and Uncle Bob had several tenant houses on their property. It took a lot of working hands to tend the cotton fields. Perhaps I would not have heard complaints anyway, but I never knew anyone to say they had been treated unfairly. When you labor side by side from sun-up to sun-down, when windstorm and hail or drought and pestilence threatens a livelihood which is planted in the common soil of a farm, you are linked by the struggles and fears you face together. A bond is formed which outsiders do not see.

Ed and his family forged such a bond. When he eventually built a house on land purchased from Uncle Bob and went on to other jobs, he was still Aunt Berta's right hand. After Uncle Bob was gone, many of her decisions were made to wait until she consulted with Ed.

Years began to take their toll on both of them and eventually Ed, whose talented wife had already died, was placed in a nursing home down the road from the farm he knew so well. His children, leaders in the community, filled in to assist Aunt Berta just as their daddy had done. Normally, Aunt Berta couldn't bear to go to the nursing facility, but she went to see Ed. She grieved that it was necessary for him to be a patient there.

One day Ed walked away from that place of care setting in motion a grand scale search. Aunt Berta and my mother, who lived in a cottage behind the big house on the farm, had no knowledge of Ed's disappearance. However, it was Mama who found him. She was taking a walk when she saw someone sitting beside a tree in the woods behind her house.

Upon investigation she discovered it was Ed. Bless his heart, he was all tired out from his walk, but he was happy. He had come home, home to where he had spent many hours driving the tractor or helping with the cows.

Mama and Aunt Berta helped him up and Mama cooked him a substantial breakfast. I don't know who was the happiest, my two elderly loved ones or Ed, who was more like family than he was friend. It was touching to hear how glad they were to see him. Relieved they could call his children with news that he was okay, they were also saddened that it was necessary for him to return for the care his body required. In the interim they all enjoyed a few precious moments together.

You can't find any greater love and appreciation than that. Not one of the three cared a whit that their skin color was a little different from the other. They had always watched out for each other. Age had only strengthened what they shared.

Would he have chosen that place to come to if he had memories of being treated in any way but with respect?

When in 2003 fire destroyed my farm buildings, it was family members of long-ago tenant farmers of Uncle Bob's, who came to clean up and cart off. It was Homer with his huge bulldozer, who just as he leveled the charred earth, smoothed some of the despair and grief in my spirit.

I see Liza in my childhood memory standing at the ironing board with a smile on her cheerful face, Liza, whom I would never dream of sassing or not minding what she said.

Then there is Annie Lou, who lived in one of Aunt Berta's tenant houses and took care of the laundry and the house. When

I brought Aunt Berta home from the hospital to die it was Annie Lou who came on the bus from Atlanta to help me take care of my aunt and her friend. It was my mama and Annie Lou who stood by her bedside when Aunt Berta drew her last breath.

The Reverend James H. Miller is an astounding bundle of energy, often referred to as the Pastor At Large in our county. Although pastor of two churches, he ministers to the entire community as well. In our family, as well as in many others, his mighty prayers have upheld us with strength and hope. For many years he has appeared when our need was great.

As I look down the corridors of those years, I see black and white blended together in strong and meaningful ways. As bad as some mistreatment was, and acknowledging indignities one placed upon the other, not all of our past history was the dark picture it has been painted to be. Respect, appreciation and love were woven through many of those lives in ways we cannot deny. Even separated by the rules and laws of that time, there was still an irrevocable tie that binds the people of the South as we knew it, in a way I never saw in our northernmost counterpart.

✻✺⟨⚥⟩✺✻

"Our Father, it is not the sins of another generation for which we can ask forgiveness, but that of our own. Grant us the wisdom to always be fair in our dealings with fellow travelers in this life. We know muddied waters have crossed the roads of the past…our part is to learn from them. Thank you for the distinctiveness of each race that you have created. Help us to honor and care for those who walk beside us along the way."

Chapter 56
The Prayer of Protection

In the book of Job, Satan asks God a question concerning His servant, Job, "Have you not made a hedge about him and his house and all that he has, on every side?" (Job 1:10 KJV). Throughout Scripture we are given illustrations of God's hedges of protection. Is it not reasonable to believe that as believers we have the right to request those hedges of God? I believe not only do we have the right, but we can be given an urgent charge to pray circles of protection around our loved ones. An experience I had when my children were young impressed this fact upon me quite strongly.

Wayne was in his early teens when he and a visiting friend were roaming around the woods on our farm. Inside our house, I was calmly reading when suddenly as if a siren went off in my head, I knew something was seriously wrong. It centered around Wayne, not his friend, and I felt the same urgency I experienced when I was summoned to Lena's. I tried to reason with myself, that I had a big imagination, that my son would be embarrassed if I went running to find them. Besides, I had no idea which direction they had taken.

The gravity of the situation did not leave me, so I began to pray for his safety with no inkling as to what threatened him. I prayed a hedge of protection around him, asking God to deliver him from whatever danger he might be in.

I hurried outside to determine what I might do next, when I saw Wayne and his friend coming up the road, with Wayne clutching his arm. At the pond on adjoining land Wayne had taken a tumble on the dam and broken his elbow. Of course it required a trip to the hospital, but it was fixable.

Later, I went over the events in my mind. Why was I given this warning? He had fallen anyway. Was he in far greater danger when I was alerted to pray? We have no answers to such situations, but it does give me thought as to protection we may receive yet never know about. Are the angels really all around us, guarding and protecting? Do our prayers actually place our loved ones under a safer umbrella? I choose to believe they do.

In more recent years, Brenda and I both had a night of praying for this son when he was on his way to Georgia.

After living in the D.C. and Maryland area for twenty years, Wayne decided to move back to the farm. He had already brought one truck full of office equipment and unloaded it in the basement of my mother's house. He flew back to Bethesda and loaded another large rental truck with all else that he owned in this world.

It had been practically a non-stop pack and load week. He left Maryland late in the day, having just finished packing the truck. Already bone weary he set out alone on the long drive to Georgia. Later he would make a return trip to pick up his van and his fiance.

Brenda had come to spend the night at my house and we had worked all afternoon getting his house clean and ready for occupation. We were asleep at around 1:30 in the morning when the phone rang. Somehow, a phone ringing in the wee hours of the night has an ominous sound. It was not good news. Wayne was somewhere on a lonely stretch of road in the middle of North Carolina with a blown engine.

The call came from a truck stop he had found after a two mile walk along a particularly unpopulated stretch of road. When the truck came to a grinding halt, he had to leave it with all his earthly possessions, and walk until he found some place from which to call, not knowing how far that might be but reasoning he would find it eventually. By the time he called me, he had already called the rental company, who promised to send help as soon as possible. He confided to me his fear upon returning to the truck that all his furniture might be gone.

That was the news Brenda and I had to digest. I think we both began to imagine the worst — the what if's. What if robbers were at the truck when he got there? What if everything was gone? What if they hurt him or worse, killed him?

The what if's completely leave out trust. We soon came to our senses and remembered we had the greatest power in the world to protect Wayne and his belongings.

We began to pray the prayer of protection, that God would build a hedge around him to keep him from harm. When at last we found a peace through relinquishing our loved one to God's keeping, we were able to sleep.

The next morning brought news that the rental company had rescued him, put him up for the night, and ordered another vehicle which they loaded. It took all day and he left Charlotte, North Carolina about five o'clock that evening. He still had several hundred miles ahead of him, but this time he was rested.

Brenda stayed the night again and we sat up late, listening to the heavy rain against the windows. We knew he towed a trailer behind the truck because the men couldn't get it packed as closely as Wayne had. After eleven o'clock we began to get anxious but finally we heard the heavy motor of a big truck laboring up the rain slick hill to our house. It was the most wonderful sound in the world. He was here at last and safe!

Whether the great need for prayer comes through inner warning, or through learning the news in other ways, I believe we are shown such needs for a reason. It is a grace warning that presents us an opportunity to intercede on behalf of that person.

Again, it is that which I do not fully comprehend about the whys and wherefores when I know God watches over us anyway. But I firmly believe there is some sort of extra power granted when we are "heavenly counseled" to pray a prayer of protection.

✳ ✦❨✥❩✦ ✳

"Dear God, I am grateful for those times You send messengers to alert me of impending doom with summons to special and essential prayer. I don't have to understand it to be obedient. It makes unseen curves in the road less fearful and more approachable."

Chapter 57
Emmanuel

Kenny Heath, our minister of education, asked if I would take the Sunday school class of my peers, a couples class my age; some a little older, some younger. Good heavens, no! I would never attempt to teach a class of folk who knew a lot more than me. No siree, I did not want to do it. I was sure God didn't want me to do it either. Plainly it was the nominating committee's idea.

Then Kenny asked me if I would pray about it. Well, what could I say but yes, I could do that. I knew, however, what my answer would be.

It's not that I had never served in such capacity before. Over most of my adult life, I had been called Sunday school teacher of varied classes from youngest to oldest. It would not have been the first class of adult couples I ever led either. The truth is I never felt qualified to be called teacher. Leader of some sort maybe, but I was not trained as a teacher. However, most churches are so glad for anybody to take this volunteer job that credentials of education are not required, only credentials of Christianity.

I promised I'd pray about it. I thought that would settle it for me, and when I would call Kenny to refuse, it would settle the whole matter, period.

I entered my first session of prayer pertaining to the situation, honestly seeking. At the same time, I told God I felt it was not right for me and surely He would agree. That would lay it to rest and I would have peace about it.

But the peace I expected did not come. I let it idle for a day or so, after which I began to give God excuses. I am not qualified, I'm tired, I have served my time.

When He began to wake me in the night to speak to my heart, I listened. When I said "I'm not qualified," He said, "Then, you will look to me." When I complained about not having the energy, He said, "At your weakest, then it is My strength." When I said I had done enough, He said, "I am to be served forever."

I struggled with disturbing indecision for few days. Then I listed all the Lord had done for me, especially the last few years. It was when I got to the time after my husband's death I remembered most clearly the personal comfort of our Lord Jesus, Himself.

The first fall when I was adjusting to the lostness of being alone, hurricane Opal came roaring inland from the Gulf Coast. Seldom does the backlash of hurricanes bother us with more than stronger winds than usual and rain. This time, however, the force as it blew its way northward was tremendous. Preparing for bed that night, the minute by minute news reports of coming disaster was enough to scare the bravest.

I crawled between the covers, fearful and worried, and asked God to protect us through the night. I imagined I would spend sleepless hours. I hoped I would have time to go to the basement if need be. I slept.

Not only did I sleep, I rested completely undisturbed. I was wrapped in a protective cocoon and had not heard the fury of the winds as they tore through the farm. When I awoke to morning light, the storm had long gone. Further inspection showed several huge oaks a few yards up the road from my house toppled to the ground. It had to have created a tremendous noise. My yard was strewn with limbs and debris but the trees surrounding my house were still standing.

Normally I am not such a sound sleeper. I sensed divine protection and felt blessed beyond measure. When I have needed strength, Jesus has given it. When I have coveted guidance, He has shown the way. When I began to look at all the present help I receive in many situations, I asked myself, how could I not be obedient? If a Bible class is what He required of me, I would do the best I could.

This is my fifth year attempting to do what has become a special segment of my life. I refer to myself as Bible study leader rather than teacher. For the most part the wonderful group of men and women in the Emmanuel class teach me. They serve our Lord through ministering and caring for each other, and their generous spirits have enfolded me with love and support.

In the class we share joys and woes with each other. We pray one another through illnesses, and tests, and surgeries. We comfort each other in grief and tribulation. We laugh at ourselves and worry about our children and grandchildren together. We discuss issues and attempt to solve problems. We have fellowship together with feasts and outings. We respect each person's privacy and we praise and worship our God, who is with us.

To Kenny, who asked me to pray about it, and to each of these special ones, some of whom have come and gone, I am eternally grateful...Doc, A.O. and Jean, Bernice and James, Dot and Charles, Joan and Virgil, Bob and Kathy, Bill and Hazel, Ray and Wilma, Lillian and Earl, Alice and Dewey, Peggy and Tommy, Sarah, Laurenze and Lloyd, Dorothy and Randy, Ann and

Raymond, Earl W. and Opal, Myrtle, Charlotte and Merrell, Mac and Louise, Doris, Alma and Charles, Miriam, and Jim.

Named by Nan Gardner Brown, our class is Emmanuel, God with us. He is indeed that. He is with each of us, and with all of us.

"I marvel, Lord Jesus, at how You bring certain people into our lives and how You place us where we need to be in Your plan of things. Please continue to bless these special ones and give them strong evidence of Your walk with them, as we all continue on this last segment of the Emmaus Road."

Chapter 58
Last Things

When I fed Boomer in the little house where I stored canning jars, he wanted to go back outside after he ate. But I closed the door of "Boomer's house." I secured the latch and left him there, this special black and white bowling ball of a cat who had appeared years ago out of nowhere. It would be the last time I shut his door.

When I started to the house I passed Molly, the tortoiseshell, who was asking to be let into the cycle shed. It was where we parked our lawn mower and the three wheeler. I let Molly into her favorite place and locked the door. It would be for the last time.

I fed Siam, our Siamese, and Rennie and Bart, the black shorthairs, in one of the barn's bays where they always ate. It would be the last time I would feed them there.

I moved on to the farm shop and situated Orange, who was ancient and needed a warm bed, and Cletu, who felt safest with his buddy. I locked the shop door for the last time. I felt better with the cats inside at night, or at least in the barn area where they could quickly get to safety. Coyotes, natural predators of cats, ranged all around us.

The dogs had a large enclosed room in the barn with an open bay joined to their pen. When I went to feed them, they were frightened by the threatening sound of distant rumbles. They begged to return to the house with me. For reasons I didn't know I gave in to their plea. I closed the barn door for the last time.

I speak of things I did for the last time. I did not die, but as I relive that night I have to admit a part of me did. Strange, how we can do last things without any warning that we will never do those things again.

The thunder had intensified with violent lightning. The storm went on and on. Finally, I went to bed around 11:30. It was one A.M. when I awakened from a deep sleep and saw the light on my bedroom wall. My first thought was that I had failed to turn out a lamp.

When I stepped from my room a great wall of fire met my horrified gaze. The barn was in full flame! The shop, merely feet away, had not caught at that point. I rushed in and got Orange out but I couldn't find Cletu and left the door open so he could escape.

By the time the fire fighters got here and rolled out their hoses, the shop was also in flames. Miraculously, my house—not fifty feet away—was not even smudged by the smoke or tremendous heat.

We lost everything in the barn: tractors, ton-and-a-half truck, much farm machinery, the antique farm equipment I'd hoped to give to the county museum when it was ready, plus all the power tools in the shop. The worst loss for me was the cats. I grieved that it was I who closed the doors upon them, but three of them not enclosed also died. Did they hide in the only sanctuary they knew?

I was grateful I had no large farm animals to perish. I am profoundly thankful for Tom and his wonderful fire crew that kept the flames from my house, and that I had brought the dogs to the house for the night. Their outside enclosure was not large enough for them to escape from the tremendous inferno.

While I grieved for what I had lost, I began to count my blessings. To me, it was no small miracle that I was awakened soon after going into that first deep sleep pattern. The house could have been consumed with all its inhabitants inside, but a force field seemed to surround us. Had angels held hands to protect us?

My vehicles were damaged but could be repaired. My brave son had arrived early enough to run into the car shelter and back them out before the shelter began to burn in earnest.

People came in surprising numbers to help us clean up the burned and charred debris left from the 150 x 40 foot structure of six open bays and four enclosed rooms. We were able to rebuild on a much smaller scale, and unbelievably in two months it was done. Since that fateful night when lightning lanced down with such devastation, I have thought a lot about last things. On the day we take our leave for eternity, we will have done some last things. Throughout our lives we perform certain acts for others, for family and friends, which we will never do again.

Can we look back and believe we handled it rightly and well, that we did the best we could with what we were given? It made me aspire to consider each occasion and person important enough to ask myself: if this is the last time I perform this service will I have no regrets? It made me want to live each day in such a way that will honor in greater fashion this Lord Jesus with whom I am privileged to walk the Emmaus Road.

⚜

"My gratitude knows no end, Lord, when I relive that fearful night and realize how strongly we were protected. You know my grief at the loss of loved pets, and my human feeling concerning the loss of things. You remind me how things are for our use, and not to be glorified. Thank You for shielding us from flames of harm and hurt and loss."

Chapter 59
Standing in the Gap

I pulled the envelope from the mail box. It was a bread recipe from my son-in-law I had requested because his loaves were lighter than mine. That was Ric, always ready to help you in whatever way he could. He sort of stands in the gap and when there is a need he fills it.

At various times he has helped out on the farm. City boy that he is, I am sure surprises often met him. Like the time he told Edwin he would help pick up potatoes. By the look on his face when he saw the potatoes the plow had unearthed, I think he pictured a few pounds rather than many bushels.

It was Ric with his woodwork ability who restored the wooden glider Edwin had made for my mother years earlier. Once Ric deftly repaired the worn part, he suggested we place it on the front porch for more protection from the elements.

Edwin had also made a little white picket fence to separate the drive from the yard. It saddened me to see it falling apart and Brenda and I talked of what we could do to replace it. It depressed me to look at it. It seemed so many things Edwin had created were disappearing.

Ric came one day to help clean salvaged tools with the pressure washer he borrowed from his son, Chris. He brought his son-in-law Paul, an efficient and powerful worker. Ric took note of the fallen fence, but Ric-like, he didn't say much.

A few weeks later he returned in his van with his own special fence design, and began to assemble the pieces. It's a low rustic style, the perfect solution to dividing the yard from the drive area.

Soon after, he brought back a table which we had used outside for vegetable sorting. Previously, it sat under the huge oak nearest the barn and was burned on one side from the fire. With a metal top, it had been extremely useful and I lamented that our table was gone. Ric took it home, replaced the destroyed areas and painted it white. Brenda and I decided it was more useful in the newly erected shop and too nice to place outside, so now it is an essential fixture in our farm shop beside the workbench he built for us.

Ric quietly ferreted away tools whose handles had burned. What was returned was a shovel, a rake, an ax, and my favorite hoe all newly painted with brand new handles.

This past spring he secured PVC pipe for a deer fence Brenda had dreamed up. It didn't matter that they were bright blue. With the new plan Brenda had concocted we got the fence in place, which worked quite well to keep the intruders out of our corn patch that year. Ric is always ready to listen to our wild schemes and do what he can to aid them, as well as finding buyers for our extra produce.

While I am decorating or preparing for the holiday seasons, I am often accompanied by a tape of my son-in-law's music. He is a gifted pianist and organist. Then I am reminded of his ability in the kitchen. It wouldn't seem like Christmas and Thanksgiving without the wonderful salad Ric brings to our family meals every year.

Often in life it is the small things tumbled together that multiplies them into larger significance. It is comforting to know that whenever there is a need, someone like Ric is ready to fill in the gap and in some meaningful way make the way easier for those in their midst.

"When we set out on life's journey, Father, we have no idea who will travel with us. But You do. You know far ahead who will be our family members and who will be those our children bring into the family. It is the pattern of things You ordained long ago — the family unit. We praise You for it."

Chapter 60
Choices

I got off the four-wheeler and let another dog out for the morning run. This time it was Ginger, her coat of bronze shining in the morning sun. She looked a picture against the spring green grass covering the barn yard.

It has been four years since the fire when the same spot was black and charred. I marvel how it is a pleasant place again. I can remember it now without falling apart. I can think of the wonderful people who came and made all the devastation disappear. Homer and his brother Willie James, who had known me since my teens, brought heavy equipment and a crew of men. Eddie, Horace, from my church Raymond, Tommy, and Beth, men from my son-in-law's firm, and my neighbor Steven, all came to do what they could. They sorted, salvaged, hauled and bulldozed the debris away.

The day after the fire when we were still numb with shock and didn't realize we were hungry, Opal, Alice, Ramona, Betty, and Jean came with the traditional help that women have been offering since time began. They brought us food.

Each time we use the air compressor or some of the other

tools, I am overwhelmed by the generosity of my Sunday school class who provided some of them.

Rick, Gerald, and JT took the pickup and repaired its burned front so I would have an immediate means of transportation. Gratitude fills my heart when I think of those so willing to give of themselves.

During barn and shop rebuilding Brenda bore most of the burden with help from her brother when he could give it. On the day we were to move supplies stored in the rented container to the newly constructed shop I was useless, having been diagnosed with Lyme Disease. So Brenda, with nothing more than moral support from Rusty the cat, moved countless cartloads of salvaged tools, materials and cabinets by herself.

For weeks after the fire, whenever I lay down and closed my eyes, all I could see were the flames. I would lie still, the shock sweeping through me again and again. Why had I not awakened sooner? I could see me closing the doors where I thought the cats would be safe from coyotes. I could see familiar objects that were no more, and once again experience our loss. I had been a steward of irreplaceable antique farm equipment the great-grandparents had left, of my husband's machinery and power tools, and I had failed them.

Then one day I was stopped with a reminder: you have a choice. A choice? Once an older friend, Mae, and I were discussing how things happen to us over which we have no control. She told me that we can wallow in whatever our less than perfect circumstance happens to be. But we have a choice. We can choose not to dwell upon the negative.

I know now it was the Holy Spirit's way of helping me deal with my losses. Every time the horror of that night came to me, I made a deliberate choice not to entertain those thoughts.

Instead, I would picture a better time, and banish from my mind the unhealthy, unwholesome scenes of destruction.

I still must maintain that preventive practice, for sometimes the flames threaten to engulf me. Then I remember I can make a choice. In all of life's decisions and happenings we have choices to make.

We choose which college to attend, which career to follow, which person to marry, where to live. The greatest choice we ever make is: will I follow Jesus, God's Son, or another?

Our well-being hangs on our choices. Where we spend eternity is made by our choice. Jesus or another?

***

"Long ago I chose You, Lord Jesus, when all I understood was that You invited me to come. Your Word has promised we can come to You as a little child with mere child-like understanding, and You will welcome us. Then I lacked spiritual knowledge, but I knew one thing. You were my choice, and it was enough."

Chapter 61
The We of Me

Recently Brenda and I traveled to Tennessee to attend the wedding of one of our cousins. It seems more and more that we only see those who live at a distance either at funerals or weddings. I was grateful this was a happy occasion.

After the vows had been made in the beautiful church setting, we traveled to a posh downtown hotel for the reception. Most of the family stayed over and we breakfasted together the next morning before parting ways to different destinations...some to Florida, Texas, Georgia, or Alabama, and the rest to other parts of Tennessee.

At one point in the festivities I sat aside and watched the very young ones play with cousins they had not seen in a while. I felt a sudden closeness to Nannie and Granddaddy and wished they could see these robust little persons, who were their great-great-great grandchildren. It didn't seem possible that in my lifetime I had lived to see the sixth generation of this family. These little ones would never know those who came before them. I hoped one day they might be inspired to find how we all fit together.

Family connections are important. Much evidence of the

importance of genealogy is in the Bible, but many are not interested in the begots. While present day, this moment, is all we really have, it matters that many came before us and tracked the way if in no other manner save through blood and genes. If they had not come first we would not be here either.

I write this because I want these cousins to know their heritage, their beginnings, their lineage. It is to the generation before them that I attempted in a previous chapter to explain our relationship. To these young ones I write about here, I am third cousin thrice removed.

I want them to know the unselfishness of those great-great-great grandparents whom I tell about throughout this book. I hope they will always know the joy of family, the unit the Heavenly Father created at time's beginning.

Even though families have changed with divorce, separation, and even living together as a common thing, it is still a unit that God established at the birth of mankind. So it does matter who we are, and how we relate to the nucleus of our being.

We all know just as there are good and honorable families, sadly there also exist those where children grow up in misery and abuse. When I hear of circumstances like that, I realize anew that I was so very fortunate that Nannie and Granddaddy opened their hearts to enfold my mother and then me into the sanctuary of their home. By no great ado we were made immediate family.

I think of the upright, decent men in my young life: Granddaddy, Jack, Nelson, and Uncle Bob, all who treated me not only with kindness, but with protection. No harm would ever befall me as long as these valiant gentlemen watched over me.

While cousins may not mean much in large families with many brothers and sisters and parents still alive, in cases such as ours cousins are all we have left of a family line.

My prayer is that the great, the great-great, and the great-great-

great-grand children on down the line of these third and four removed cousins in our family will be as protected and blessed. For those of you who read, may yours be protected as well.

※❀❀❀❀

"In your plan of family and connections, Lord, thank you for those who came before us to smooth the trodden path that we have traveled. May we leave a clean and clear passage for those who follow."

Chapter 62
The Road Ahead

I considered calling this chapter Journey's End, but since my walk has not ended I can still look forward to what is ahead. At the same time, because of my age I am strongly aware that I am a lot closer to the end than I am to the beginning.

At a certain point in my life, I was impressed to look down the road I had traveled thus far and to review my mental and spiritual bearings. Along those places and through those experiences, I saw Jesus. My eyes did not pick up His being in the same way I see this page before me. My soul saw Him, my heart saw Him, the inner place where the Holy Spirit abides in me connected with Him so emphatically there is no denying He is very present in our midst.

On some occasions wherever I was in time, I realized He was nearby. Other times I didn't recognize Him until later, just like the two who walked with Him toward Emmaus immediately after His resurrection. Walking with Jesus is an overwhelming experience. In writing about the people who have traveled with me in and out of my winding path, gratitude overflows for those who lightened burdens I might have born alone. Yesterday I found a letter in a big Bible my mother had given me. It was written seventy-six years ago by Aunt Berta, my daddy's only sister. Mama, Daddy, and I had been visiting at the family homeplace in Georgia where Aunt Berta and Uncle Bob lived with my grandmother, who at the time was seventy-two. I was the only grandchild and the end of the family line.

In her articulate style my beloved Aunt Berta described the emptiness of the house once we had returned to Ohio. Throughout the letter you could feel the love emanating from the pages. She voiced the loneliness they felt because of the absence of chubby one-year-old me. She spoke of the concern Daddy experienced at leaving his mother, wondering at her age if he would ever see her again.

These are normal worries when families are separated by distance and strong confirmation that we have no idea where the road ahead will carry us. My grandmother lived twenty more years, and my father died four years after the letter was written.

Even when we are oblivious to the truth that God has a plan for our life, I believe He guides our way. After Daddy died, Mama and I were given a home in Ohio with Nannie and Granddaddy. And I, eventually in Georgia with my grandmother, Aunt Berta, and Uncle Bob. Except for them my route might have taken a completely different direction, and though all of them are gone from this realm, I am still sustained by their love.

My hope has been that if you read my unremarkable story it will cause you to look down your own Emmaus Road, and remember. Recall the times when there was no human explanation of your circumstances. Allow those memories to help you see the reality of Jesus and how He longs for your perception of Him beside you as you travel the years of your life. Remembrances of the past can help us appreciate and use the present in more beneficial ways.

I believe it is important to recognize your responsibility that as you walk, you mark a trail. As never before in the United States, many sorts of beliefs exist. Some scoff and ridicule Christianity, and desire to do away with any reminder of it.

Recently a gentle Hindu man spoke to me of his tenet: that we are all the same, that all religions are the same, that God was present long before Christ.

As he talked, I nodded and listened to him. I agreed that God was known long before Christ appeared on the earthly scene, but we Christians believe that God the Father chose a precise time to send Jesus the Son to bridge the gap between us. Knowing that mankind could never find the way to Holy God without an unblemished Savior, He sent a marvelous gift of His love for us: God Himself in the human Presence of Jesus…God with us.

I wanted to say more, but the gentleman walked away. I wanted to say, yes, I believe we are all the same in how God loves each of us, but no, I do not believe all religions are the same. I wanted to tell him Jesus is not a religion. Jesus is a Person who will walk beside you if you will allow it.

God gave us free will. I honor that, but if I tell you this is what I believe, my prayer is that it might in some way help you to find the inner joy acceptance will bring. We need to completely understand that we either accept the Son of God or we reject Him. There is no middle road. The heart, mind, and spirit are all involved. It is our minds that first receive the truth: if we accept Jesus we will know God. But that is not far enough; even the demons believe and tremble, and continue on their wayward path.

Faith helps us to believe what our minds receive. With complete clarity we see the cross where Jesus paid the ransom for any who turn to Him and seek forgiveness. We invite the Person, Jesus, into our hearts—into our inner being. The transaction is then sealed by the Holy Spirit, who comes within to be our Helper, our Guide. It is forever.

I so much want the people I love to know for themselves this truth which would secure them for eternity. My heart grieved when I couldn't convince every one. I have prayed and prayed about my lack, my inability to help them understand.

That's where I was one bitter winter day when I walked a familiar woods path with the dogs. I asked God's guidance, begging Him to show me how to approach those who would not listen. What could I say that would remove the scales from their eyes, and thaw hardened hearts? Why didn't I have a magic touch which would make them see?! What Scripture could I point them toward?

Pouring out these questions aloud to God, I cried. "What proof do I have, God, that Christ is real? If they don't believe in the authenticity of Your Holy Word, what proof do we have?"

As I stepped from the protection of the woods, icy blasts of wind hit me head-on, chilling the tears on my face. At that exact moment, clearly and with great authority I heard the words, "The proof is in you!"

In me, in inadequate, hopeless me? There was no mistaking the message. It shook the foundation of my soul when I thoroughly understood I would never have a special touch, no distinctive ability. It was not me at all, but He who lived within me. The proof is in the Holy Spirit of the Lord Jesus Christ. We are not called to be successful; we are called to simply share our story. The rest is up to the Holy Spirit. The evidence is in all the "you's," all believers who have invited Him into their hearts.

He will embrace everyone who will allow it. He never forces or coerces. He waits for you to reach out to Him, and He will meet you more than halfway. Your life will never be the same.

When Jesus left this earth and ascended into heaven, His

command was: go and tell others. This is what I have tried to do here. This is my story.

"As they talked and discussed these things with each other, Jesus himself came up and walked with them; but they were kept from recognizing Him… Then their eyes were opened and they recognized him" (Luke 24:15-16,31 NIV).

May it be so with you in your walk along Emmaus.

"Holy Lord Jesus, thank You for that moment on my life's road when You turned me to look back to many reminders of Your constant Presence. It's been a breathtaking experience because You were there. Thank You for beloved ones who travel with us. My cup is full and running over. I turn my eyes that You have opened toward the rest of the journey on the Emmaus Road."